The Mystery of the Sycamore

By Carolyn Wells

Originally published in 1920

The Mystery of the Sycamore

© 2013 Resurrected Press
www.ResurrectedPress.com

Published by Resurrected Press

This classic book was handcrafted by Resurrected Press. Resurrected Press is dedicated to bringing high quality classic books back to the readers who enjoy them. These are not scanned versions of the originals, but, rather, quality checked and edited books meant to be enjoyed!

Please visit ResurrectedPress.com to view our entire catalogue!

ISBN 13: 978-1-937022-47-1

Printed in the United States of America

FOREWORD

When Carolyn Wells wrote *The Mystery of the Sycamore*, she had been writing detective stories for more than a decade and had over a dozen mysteries to her credit. Before her death in the forties, she would go on to write dozens more, becoming one of America's most popular mystery writers during the period.

This growth in experience shows in this novel, published in 1920. While her earlier works had tended to feature extremely wealthy characters who were almost caricatures, by 1920 she had begun to people her novels with characters drawn from the middle class, lawyers, doctors, and in this case politicians. The elaborate architectural puzzles involving secret passages and hidden doors that dominated her early works have also given way to more realistic methods. The focus of her works changed, too. Whereas her early mysteries usually featured a young woman oppressed by either an older husband or a restrictive guardian, it is the male characters that assume a greater role in her later books.

1920 marked the beginning of an era that was to become known as the "Golden Age" of British mysteries, a period that was dominated by Agatha Christie, Dorothy L. Sayers and others. It was a style when the puzzle of the crime was preeminent. Carolyn Wells was never as adept or interested in such puzzles, being always more interested in the interactions between her characters as following their feelings as suspicion falls on first one and then another of the suspects. Yet, Wells was not immune to the change of taste. In *The Mystery of the Sycamore* the fire in the garage that serves as a distraction to the murder is started by means that are more complicated, yet more believable, than Wells would have used earlier.

And subthemes such as the supernatural aspect of the mystery bugler are more muted that in previous books.

The Mystery of the Sycamore features that favorite detective of Wells', Fleming Stone, distinguished, reserved, unemotional. In the book he describes how there are two types of cases, the "express" and the "local." In the express cases, he shows up, usually in the last few chapters, makes a few observations, and announces the solution. The local cases provide more of a challenge, forcing the detective to show up near the middle of the book, be much more involved in actual detecting, and only reaching a solution with difficulty. This story is definitely one of the latter variety.

It is appropriate to mention here a few words about Stone's associate, Fibsy. Fibsy, or Terrence McGuire, is an Irish street urchin who makes his first appearance in *Vicky Van*. His nickname comes from his tendency to embellish the truth, a facility which proves useful when he seeks to elicit information from servants and trades people. More than just a comic foil for Stone, Fibsy conducts much of the dirty work of investigation, allowing Stone to avoid sullying either his dignity or his wardrobe. Fibsy also provides a medium for saying that which Stone would never be able to say.

With *The Mystery of the Sycamore*, Wells was hitting her stride, producing a more mature, nuanced story than in some of her earlier works. It is with pleasure that Resurrected Press brings you this new edition of *The Mystery of the Sycamore*.

About the Author

Carolyn Wells, June 18, 1862 March 26, 1942 was an American writer and poet. She was best known for her books of poetry and humor until around 1910 she read one of Anna Katherine Green's mysteries and took up the genre. Many of her mysteries featured the detective Fleming Stone. She was married to Hadwin Houghton, heir to the Houghton-Mifflin publishing company. She was a collector of poetry by other authors, and, upon her death, she bequeathed her collection of the works of Walt Witman to the Library of Congress.

Greg Fowlkes
Editor-In-Chief
Resurrected Press
www.ResurrectedPress.com

TABLE OF CONTENTS

CHAPTER 1: THE LETTER THAT SAID COME

As the character of a woman may be accurately deduced from her handkerchief, so a man's mental status is evident from the way he opens his mail.

Curtis Keefe, engaged in this daily performance, slit the envelopes neatly and laid the letters down in three piles. These divisions represented matters known to be of no great interest; matters known to be important; and, third, letters with contents as yet unknown and therefore of problematical value.

The first two piles were, as usual, dispatched quickly, and the real attention of the secretary centered with pleasant anticipation on the third lot.

"Gee whiz, Genevieve!"

As no further pearls of wisdom fell from the lips of the engrossed reader of letters, the stenographer gave him a round-eyed glance and then continued her work.

Curtis Keefe was, of course, called Curt by his intimates, and while it may be the obvious nickname was brought about by his short and concise manner of speech, it is more probable that the abbreviation was largely responsible for his habit of curtness.

Anyway, Keefe had long cultivated a crisp, abrupt style of conversation. That is, until he fell in with Samuel Appleby. That worthy ex-governor, while in the act of engaging Keefe to be his confidential secretary, observed: "They call you Curt, do they? Well, see to it that it is short for courtesy."

This was only one of several equally sound bits of advice from the same source, and as Keefe had an eye single to the glory of self-advancement, he kept all these things and pondered them in his heart.

The result was that ten years of association with Lawyer Appleby had greatly improved the young man's manner, and though still brief of speech, his curtness had lost its unpleasantly sharp edge and his courtesy had developed into a dignified urbanity, so that though still Curt Keefe, it was in name only.

"What's the pretty letter all about, Curtis?" asked the observant stenographer, who had noticed his third reading of the short missive.

"You'll probably answer it soon, and then you'll know," was the reply, as Keefe restored the sheet to its envelope and took up the next letter.

Genevieve Lane produced her vanity-case, and became absorbed in its possibilities.

"I wish I didn't have to work," she sighed; "I wish I was an opera singer."

"'Cromwell, I charge thee, fling away ambition,'" murmured Keefe, his eyes still scanning letters; "'by that sin fell the angels,' and it's true you are angelic, Viva, so down you'll go, if you fall for ambition."

"How you talk! Ambition is a good thing."

"Only when tempered by common sense and perspicacity—neither of which you possess to a marked degree."

"Pooh! You're ambitious yourself, Curt."

"With the before-mentioned qualifications. Look here, Viva, here's a line for you to remember. I ran across it in a book. 'If you do only what is absolutely correct and say only what is absolutely correct—you can do anything you like.' How's that?"

"I don't see any sense in it at all."

"No? I told you you lacked common sense. Most women do."

"Huh!" and Genevieve tossed her pretty head, patted her curly ear-muffs, and proceeded with her work.

Samuel Appleby's beautiful home graced the town of Stockfield, in the western end of the Commonwealth of Massachusetts. Former Governor Appleby was still a political power and a man of unquestioned force and importance.

It was fifteen years or more since he had held office, and now, a great desire possessed him that his son should follow in his ways, and that his beloved state should know another governor of the Appleby name.

And young Sam was worthy of the people's choice. Himself a man of forty, motherless from childhood, and brought up sensibly and well by his father, he listened gravely to the paternal plans for the campaign.

But there were other candidates, and not without some strong and definite influences could the end be attained.

Wherefore, Mr. Appleby was quite as much interested as his secretary in the letter which was in the morning's mail.

"Any word from Sycamore Ridge?" he asked, as he came into the big, cheerful office and nodded a kindly good-morning to his two assistants.

"Yes, and a good word," returned Keefe, smiling. "It says: 'Come.' "The secretary's attitude toward his employer, though deferential and respectful, was marked by a touch of good-fellowship—a not unnatural outgrowth of a long term of confidential relations between them. Keefe had made himself invaluable to Samuel Appleby and both men knew it. So, as one had no desire to presume on the fact and the other no wish to ignore it, serenity reigned in the well-ordered and well-appointed offices of the ex-governor.

Even the light-haired, light-hearted and lightheaded Genevieve couldn't disturb the even tenor of the routine. If she could have, she would have been fired.

Though not a handsome man, not even to be called distinguished looking, Samuel Appleby gave an impression of power. His strong, lean face betokened obdurate determination and implacable will.

Its deep-graven lines were the result of meeting many obstacles and surmounting most of them. And at sixty-two, the hale and hearty frame and the alert, efficient manner made the man seem years younger.

"You know the conditions on which Wheeler lives in that house?" Appleby asked, as he looked over the top of the letter at Keefe.

"No, sir."

"Well, it's this way. But, no—I'll not give you the story now. We're going down there—to-day."

"The whole tribe?" asked Keefe, briefly.

"Yes; all three of us. Be ready, Miss Lane, please, at three-thirty."

"Yes, sir," said Genevieve, reaching for her vanity-box.

"And now, Keefe, as to young Sam," Appleby went on, running his fingers through his thick, iron-gray mane. "If he can put it over, or if I can put it over for him, it will be only with the help of Dan Wheeler."

"Is Wheeler willing to help?"

"Probably not. He must be made willing. I can do it—I think—unless he turns stubborn. I know Wheeler—if he turns stubborn—well, Balaam's historic quadruped had nothing on him!"

"Does Mr. Wheeler know Sam?"

"No; and it wouldn't matter either way if he did. It's the platform Wheeler stands on. If I can keep him in ignorance of that one plank—"

"You can't."

"I know it—confound it! He opposed my election on that one point—he'll oppose Sam's for the same reason, I know."

"Where do I come in?"

"In a general way, I want your help. Wheeler's wife and daughter are attractive, and you might manage to interest them and maybe sway their sympathies toward Sam—"

"But they'll stand by Mr. Wheeler?"

"Probably—yes. However, use your head, and do all you can with it."

"And where do I come in?" asked Genevieve, who had been an interested listener.

"You don't come in at all, Miss. You mostly stay out. You're to keep in the background. I have to take you, for we're only staying one night at Sycamore Ridge, and then going on to Boston, and I'll need you there."

"Yes, sir," and the blue eyes turned from him and looked absorbedly into a tiny mirror, as Genevieve contemplated her pleasant pink-and-whiteness.

Her vanity and its accompanying box were matters of indifference to Mr. Appleby and to Keefe, for the girl's efficiency and skill outweighed them and her diligence and loyalty scored one hundred per cent.

Appleby's fetish was efficiency. He had found it and recognized it in his secretary and stenographer and he was willing to recompense it duly, even generously. Wherefore the law business of Samuel Appleby, though carried on for the benefit of a small number of clients, was of vast importance and productive of lucrative returns.

At present, the importance was overshadowed by the immediate interest of a campaign, which, if successful would land the second Appleby in the gubernatorial chair. This plan, as yet not a boom, was taking shape with the neatness and dispatch that characterized the Appleby work.

Young Sam was content to have the matter principally in his father's hands, and things had reached a pitch where, to the senior mind, the cooperation of Daniel Wheeler was imperatively necessary.

And, therefore, to Wheeler's house they must betake themselves.

"What do you know about the Wheeler business, kid?" Keefe inquired, after Mr. Appleby had left them.

Genevieve leaned back in her chair, her dimpled chin moving up and down with a pretty rhythm as she enjoyed her chewing-gum, and gazed at the ceiling beams.

Appleby's offices were in his own house, and the one given over to these two was an attractive room, fine with mahogany and plate glass, but also provided with all the paraphernalia of the most up-to- date of office furniture. There were good pictures and draperies, and a wood fire added to the cheer and mitigated the chill of the early fall weather.

Sidling from her seat, Miss Lane moved over to a chair near the fire.

"I'll take those letters when you're ready," she said. "Why, I don't know a single thing about any Wheeler. Do you?"

"Not definitely. He's a man who had an awful fight with Mr. Appleby, long ago. I've heard about him now and then, but I know no details."

"But, it seems we're to go there. Only for a night, and then, on to Boston! Won't I be glad to go!"

"We'll only be there a few days. I'm more interested in this Wheeler performance. I don't understand it. Who's Wheeler, anyhow?"

"Dunno. If Sammy turns up this morning, he may enlighten us."

Sammy did turn up, and not long after the conversation young Appleby strolled into the office.

Though still looked upon as a boy by his father, the man was of huge proportions and of an important, slightly overbearing attitude.

Somewhat like his parent in appearance, young Sam, as he was always called, had more grace and ease, if less effect of power. He smiled genially and impartially; he seemed cordial and friendly to all the world, and he was a general favorite. Yet so far he had achieved no great thing, had no claim to any especial record in public or private life.

At forty, unmarried and unattached, his was a case of an able mentality and a firm, reliable character, with no opportunity offered to prove its worth. A little more initiative and he would have made opportunities for himself; but a nature that took the line of least resistance, a philosophy that believed in a calm acceptance of things as they came, left Samuel Appleby, junior, pretty much where he was when he began. If no man could say aught against him, equally surely no man could say anything very definite for him. Yet many agreed that he was a man whose powers would develop with acquired responsibilities, and already he had a following.

"Hello, little one," he greeted Genevieve, carelessly, as he sat down near Keefe. "I say, old chap, you're going down to the Wheelers' to-day, I hear."

"Yes; this afternoon," and the secretary looked up inquiringly.

"Well, I'll tell you what. You know the governor's going there to get Wheeler's aid in my election boom, and I can tell you a way to help things along, if you agree. See?"

"Not yet, but go ahead."

"Well, it's this way. Dan Wheeler's daughter is devoted to her father. Not only filial respect and all that, but she just fairly idolizes the old man. Now, he recips, of course, and what she says goes. So—I'm asking you squarely—won't you put in a good word to Maida, that's the girl—and if you do it with your inimitable dexterity and grace, she'll fall for it."

"You mean for me to praise you up to Miss Wheeler and ask her father to give you the benefit of his influence?"

""How clearly you do put things! That's exactly what I mean. It's no harm, you know—merely the most innocent sort of electioneering—"

"Rather!" laughed Keefe. "If all electioneering were as innocent as that, the word would carry no unpleasant meaning."

"Then you'll do it?"

"Of course I will—if I get opportunity."

"Oh, you'll have that. It's a big, rambling country house—a delightful one, too—and there's tea in the hall, and tennis on the lawn, and moonlight on the verandas—"

"Hold up, Sam," Keefe warned him, "is the girl pretty?"

"Haven't seen her for years, but probably, yes. But that's nothing to you. You're working for me, you see." Appleby's glance was direct, and Keefe understood.

"Of course; I was only joking. I'll carry out your commission, if, as I said, I get the chance. Tell me something of Mr. Wheeler."

"Oh, he's a good old chap. Pathetic, rather. You see, he bumped up against dad once, and got the worst of it."

"How?"

Sam Appleby hesitated a moment and then said: "I see you don't know the story. But it's no secret, and you may as well be told. You listen, too, Miss Lane, but there's no call to tattle."

"I'll go home if you say so," Genevieve piped up, a little crisply.

"No, sit still. Why, it was while dad was governor—about fifteen years ago, I suppose. And Daniel Wheeler forged a paper—that is, he said he didn't, but twelve other good and true peers of his said he did. Anyway, he was convicted and sentenced, but father was a good friend of his, and being governor, he pardoned Wheeler. But the pardon was on condition—oh, I say—hasn't dad ever told you, Keefe?"

"Never."

"Then, maybe I'd better leave it for him to tell. If he wants you to know he'll tell you, and if not, I mustn't."

"Oh, goodness!" cried Genevieve. "What a way to do! Get us all excited over a thrilling tale, and then chop it off short!"

"Go on with it," said Keefe; but Appleby said, "No; I won't tell you the condition of the pardon. But the two men haven't been friends since, and won't be, unless the condition is removed. Of course, dad can't do it, but the present governor can make the pardon complete, and would do so in a minute, if dad asked him to. So, though he hasn't said so, the assumption is, that father expects to trade a full pardon of Friend Wheeler for his help in my campaign."

"And a good plan," Keefe nodded his satisfaction.

"But," Sam went on, "the trouble is that the very same points and principles that made Wheeler oppose my father's election will make him oppose mine. The party is the same, the platform is the same, and I can't hope that the man Wheeler is not the same stubborn, adamant, unbreakable old hickory knot he was the other time."

"And so, you want me to soften him by persuading his daughter to line up on our side?"

"Just that, Keefe. And you can do it, I am sure."

"I'll try, of course; but I doubt if even a favorite daughter could influence the man yon describe."

"Let me help," broke in the irrepressible Genevieve. "I can do lots with a girl. I can do more than Curt could. I'll chum up with her and—"

"Now, Miss Lane, you keep out of this. I don't believe in mixing women and politics."

"But Miss Wheeler's a woman."

"And I don't want her troubled with politics. Keefe here can persuade her to coax her father just through her affections—I don't want her enlightened as to any of the political details. And I can't think your influence would work half as well as that of a man. Moreover, Keefe has discernment, and if it isn't a good plan, after all, he'll know enough to discard it—while you'd blunder ahead blindly, and queer the whole game!"

"Oh, well," and bridling with offended pride, Genevieve sought refuge in her little mirror.

"Now, don't get huffy," and Sam smiled at her; "you'll probably find that Miss Wheeler's complexion is finer than yours, anyway, and then you'll hate her and won't want to speak to her at all."

Miss Lane flashed an indignant glance and then proceeded to go on with her work.

"Hasn't Wheeler tried for a pardon all this time?" Keefe asked.

"Indeed he has," Sam returned, "many times. But you see, though successive governors were willing to grant it, father always managed to prevent it. Dad can pull lots of wires, as you know, and since he doesn't want Wheeler fully pardoned, why, he doesn't get fully pardoned."

"And he lives under the stigma."

"Lots of people don't know about the thing at all. He lives—well—he lives in Connecticut—and—oh, of course, there is a certain stigma."

"And your father will bring about his full pardon if he promises—"

"Let up, Keefe; I've said I can't tell you that part—you'll get your instructions in good time. And, look here, I don't mean for you to make love to the girl. In fact, I'm told she has a suitor. But you're just to give her a little song and dance about my suitability for the election, and then adroitly persuade her to use her powers of persuasion with her stubborn father. For he will be stubborn—I know it! And there's the mother of the girl... tackle Mrs. Wheeler. Make her see that my father was justified in the course he took—and besides, he was more or less accountable to others—and use as an argument that years have dulled the old feud and that bygones ought to be bygones and all that.

"Try to make her see that a full pardon now will be as much, and in a way more, to Wheeler's credit, than if it had been given him at first—"

"I can't see that," and Keefe looked quizzical.

"Neither can I," Sam confessed, frankly, "but you can make a woman swallow anything."

"Depends on what sort of woman Mrs. Wheeler is," Keefe mused.

"I know it. I haven't seen her for years, and as I remember, she's pretty keen, but I'm banking on you to put over some of your clever work. Not three men in Boston have your ingenuity, Keefe, when it comes to sizing up a situation and knowing just how to handle it. Now don't tell father all I've said, for he doesn't especially hold with such small measures. He's all for the one big slam game, and he may be right. But I'm right, too, and you just go ahead."

"All right," Keefe agreed, "I see what you mean, and I'll do all I can that doesn't in any way interfere with your father's directions to me. There's a possibility of turning the trick through the women folks, and if I can do it, you may count on, me."

"Good! And as for you, Miss Lane, you keep in the background, and make as little mischief as you can."

"I'm not a mischief-maker," said the girl, pouting playfully, for she was not at all afraid of Sam Appleby.

"Your blue eyes and pink cheeks make mischief wherever you go," he returned; "but don't try them on Dan Wheeler. He's a morose old chap—"

"I should think he would be!" defended Genevieve; "living all these years under a ban which may, after all, be undeserved! I've heard that he was entirely innocent of the forgery!"

"Have you, indeed?" Appleby's tone was unpleasantly sarcastic. "Other people have also heard that—from the Wheeler family! Those better informed believe the man guilty, and believe, too, that my father was too lenient when he granted even a conditional pardon."

"But just think—if he was innocent—how awful his life has been all these years! You bet he'll accept the full pardon and give all his effort and influence and any possible help in return."

"Hear the child orate!" exclaimed Sam, gazing at the enthusiastic little face, as Genevieve voiced her views.

"I think he'll be ready to make the bargain, too," declared Keefe. "Your father has a strong argument. I fancy Wheeler'll jump at the chance."

"Maybe—maybe so. But you don't know how opposed he is to our principles. And he's a man of immovable convictions. In fact, he and dad are two mighty strong forces. One or the other must win out—but I've no idea which it will be."

"How exciting!" Genevieve's eyes danced. "I'm so glad I'm to go. It's a pretty place, you say?"

"Wonderful. A great sweep of rolling country, a big, long, rambling sort of house, and a splendid hospitality. You'll enjoy the experience, but remember, I told you to be good."

"I will remember," and Genevieve pretended to look cherubic.

CHAPTER 2: NORTH DOOR AND SOUTH DOOR

For Samuel Appleby to pay a visit to Daniel Wheeler was of itself an astounding occurrence. The two men had not seen each other since the day, fifteen years ago, when Governor Appleby had pardoned the convicted Wheeler, with a condition, which, though harsh, had been strictly adhered to.

They had never been friends at heart, for they were diametrically opposed m their political views, and were not of similar tastes or pursuits. But they had been thrown much together, and when the time came for Wheeler to be tried for forgery, Appleby lent no assistance to the case. However, through certain influences brought to bear, in connection with the fact that Mrs. Wheeler was related to the Applebys, the governor pardoned the condemned man, with a conditional pardon.

Separated ever since, a few letters had passed between the two men, but they resulted in no change of conditions.

As the big car ran southward through the Berkshire Hills, Appleby's thoughts were all on the coming meeting, and the scenery of autumn foliage that provoked wild exclamations of delight from Genevieve and assenting enthusiasm from Keefe left the other unmoved.

An appreciative nod and grunt were all he vouchsafed to the girl's gushing praises, and when at last they neared their destination he called her attention to a tall old sycamore tree standing alone on a ridge not far away.

"That's the tree that gives the Wheeler place its name," he informed. "Sycamore Ridge is one of the most beautiful places in Connecticut."

"Oh, are we in Connecticut?" asked Miss Lane. "I didn't know we had crossed the border. What a great old tree! Surely one of the historic trees of New England, isn't it?"

"Historic to the Wheelers," was the grim reply, and then Mr. Appleby again relapsed into silence and spoke no further word until they reached the Wheeler home.

A finely curved sweep of driveway brought them to the house, and the car stopped at the south entrance.

The door did not swing open in welcome, and Mr. Appleby ordered his chauffeur to ring the bell.

This brought a servant in response, and the visiting trio entered the house.

It was long and low, with many rooms on either side of the wide hall that went straight through from south to north. The first room to the right was a large living-room, and into this the guests were shown and were met by a grave-looking man, who neither smiled nor offered a hand as his calm gaze rested on Samuel Appleby.

Indeed, the two men stared at one another, in undisguised curiosity. Each seemed to search the other's face for information as to his attitude and intent.

"Well, Dan," Appleby said, after the silent scrutiny, "you've changed some, but you're the same good-looking chap you always were."

Wheeler gave a start and pulled himself together.

"Thank you. I suppose I should return the compliment."

"But you can't conscientiously do it, eh?" Appleby laughed. "Never mind. Personal vanity is not my besetting sin. This is my secretary, Mr. Keefe, and my assistant, Miss Lane."

"Ah, yes, yes. How are you? How do you do? My wife and daughter will look after the young lady. Maida!"

As if awaiting the call, a girl came quickly in from the hall followed by an older woman. Introductions followed, and if there was an air of constraint on the part of the host the ladies of the family showed none. Sunny-faced Maida Wheeler, with her laughing brown eyes and gold brown hair, greeted the visitors with charming cordiality, and her mother was equally kind and courteous.

Genevieve Lane's wise and appraising eyes missed no point of appearance or behavior.

"Perfect darlings, both of them!" she commented to herself. "Whatever ails the old guy, it hasn't bitten them. Or else—wait a minute—"

Genevieve was very observant—"perhaps they're putting on a little. Is their welcome a bit extra, to help things along?"

Yet only a most meticulous critic could discern anything more than true hospitality in the attitude of Mrs. Wheeler or Maida. The latter took Genevieve to the room prepared for her and chatted away in girlish fashion.

"The place is so wonderful!" Genevieve exclaimed, carefully avoiding personal talk. "Don't you just adore it?"

"Oh, yes. I've loved Sycamore Ridge for nearly fifteen years."

"Have you lived here so long?" Genevieve was alert for information. It was fifteen years ago that the pardon had been granted.

But as Maida merely assented and then changed the subject, Miss Lane was far too canny to ask further questions.

With a promptness not entirely due to chance, the stenographer came downstairs dressed for dinner some several minutes before the appointed hour. Assuming her right as a guest, she wandered about the rooms.

The south door, by which they had entered, was evidently the main entrance, but the opposite, or north door, gave on to an even more beautiful view, and she stepped out on the wide veranda and gazed admiringly about. The low ridge nearby formed the western horizon, and the giant sycamore, its straight branches outlined against the fading sunset, was impressive and a little weird. She strolled on, and turned the corner the better to see the ridge. The veranda ran all round the house, and as she went on along the western side, she suddenly became aware of a silent figure leaning against a pillar at the southwest corner.

"It is so quiet it frightens me," she said to Daniel Wheeler, as she neared him.

"Do you feel that way, too?" he asked, looking at her a little absently. "It is the lull before the storm."

"Oh, that sunset doesn't mean rain," Genevieve exclaimed, smiling, "unless your Connecticut blue laws interpret weather signs differently from our Massachusetts prophets. We are in Connecticut, aren't we?"

"Yes," and Wheeler sighed unaccountably. "Yes, Miss Lane, we are. That sycamore is the finest tree in the state."

"I can well believe it. I never saw such a grandfather of a tree! It's all full of little balls."

"Yes, buttonballs, they are called. But note its wonderful symmetry, its majestic appearance—"

"And strength! It looks as if it would stand there forever!"

"Do you think so?" and the unmistakable note of disappointment in the man's tone caused Genevieve to look up in astonishment. "Well, perhaps it will," he added quickly.

"Oh, no, of course it won't really! No tree stands forever. But it will be here long after you and I are gone."

"Are you an authority on trees?" Wheeler spoke without a smile.

"Hardly that; but I was brought up in the country, and I know something of them. Your daughter loves the country, too."

"Oh, yes—we all do."

The tone was courteous, but the whole air of the man was so melancholy, his cheerfulness so palpably assumed, that Genevieve felt sorry for him, as well as inordinately curious to know what was the matter.

But her sympathy was the stronger impulse, and with a desire to entertain him, she said, "Come for a few steps in the garden, Mr. Wheeler, won't you? Come and show me that quaint little summer-house near the front door. It is the front door, isn't it? It's hard to tell."

"Yes, the north door is the front door," Wheeler said slowly, as if repeating a lesson. "The summer-house you mention is near the front door. But we won't visit that now. Come this other way, and I'll show you a Japanese tea-house, much more attractive."

But Genevieve Lane was sometimes under the spell of the Imp of the Perverse.

"No, no," she begged, smilingly, "let the Japanese contraption wait; please go to the little summer-house now. See, how it fairly twinkles in the last gleams of the setting sun! What is the flower that rambles all over it? Oh, do let's go there now! Come, please!"

With no reason for her foolish insistence save a whim, Genevieve was amazed to see the look of fury that came over her host's face,

"Appleby put you up to that!" he cried, in a voice of intense anger. "He told you to ask me to go to that place!"

"Why, Mr. Wheeler," cried the girl, almost frightened, "Mr. Appleby did nothing of the sort! Why should he! I'm not asking anything wrong, am I? Why is it so dreadful to want to see an arbor instead of a tea-house? You must be crazy!"

When Miss Lane was excited, she was quite apt to lose her head, and speak in thoughtless fashion.

But Mr. Wheeler didn't seem to notice her informality of speech. He only stared at her as if he couldn't quite make her out, and then he suddenly seemed to lose interest in her or her wishes, and with a deep sigh, he turned away, and fell into the same brooding posture as when she had first approached him.

"Come to dinner, people," called Maida's pretty voice, as, with outstretched hands she came toward them.

"Why, dads, what are you looking miserable about? What have you done to him, Miss Lane?"

"Maida, child, don't speak like that! Miss Lane has been most kindly talking to me, of—of the beauties of Sycamore Ridge."

"All right, then, and forgive me, Miss Lane. But you see, the sun rises and sets for me in one Daniel Wheeler, Esquire, and any shadow on his face makes me apprehensive of its cause."

Only for an instant did Genevieve Lane's sense of justice rise in revolt, then her common sense showed her the better way, and she smiled pleasantly and returned:

"I don't blame you, Miss Wheeler. If I had a father, I should feel just the same way, I know. But don't do any gory-lock-shaking my way. I assure you I didn't really scold him. I only kicked because he wouldn't humor my whim for visiting the summer-house with the blossoms trailing over it! Was that naughty of me?"

But though Genevieve listened for the answer, none came.

"Come on in to dinner, daddy, dear," Maida repeated. "Come, Miss Lane, they're waiting for us."

Dinner was a delightful occasion.

Daniel Wheeler, at the head of his own table, was a charming host, and his melancholy entirely disappeared as the talk ran along on subjects grave or gay, but of no personal import.

Appleby, too, was entertaining, and the two men, with Mrs. Wheeler, carried on most of the conversation, the younger members of the party being by what seemed common consent left out of it.

Genevieve looked about the dining-room, with a pleased interest. She dearly loved beautiful appointments and was really imagining herself mistress of just such a house, and visioning herself at the head of such a table. The long room stretched from north to south, parallel with the hall, though not adjoining. The table was not in the centre, but toward the southern end, and Mr.

Wheeler, at the end near the windows, had Keefe and Miss Lane on either side of him.

Appleby, as guest of honor, sat at Mrs. Wheeler's right, and the whole effect was that of a formal dinner party, rather than a group of which two were merely office employees.

"It is one of the few remaining warm evenings," said Mrs. Wheeler, as she rose from the table, "we will have our coffee on the veranda. Soon it will be too cool for that."

"Which veranda?" asked Genevieve of Maida, as they went through the hall. "The north one, I hope."

"Your hopes must be dashed," laughed the other, "for it will be the south one. Come along."

The two girls, followed by Keefe, took possession of a group of chairs near Mrs. Wheeler, while the two older men sat apart, and soon became engrossed in their own discussions.

Nor was it long before Samuel Appleby and his host withdrew to a room which opened on to that same south veranda, and which was, in fact, Mr. Wheeler's den.

"Well, Sam," Keefe heard the other say, as he drew down the blind, "we may as well have it out now. What are you here for?"

Outwardly placid, but almost consumed with curiosity, Curt Keefe changed his seat for one nearer the window of the den. He hoped to hear the discussion going on inside, but was doomed to disappointment, for though the murmuring of the voices was audible, the words were not distinct, and Keefe gathered only enough information to be sure that there was a heated argument in progress and that neither party to it was inclined to give in a single point.

Of course, he decided, the subject was the coming election campaign, but the details of desired bargaining he could not gather.

Moreover, often, just as he almost heard sentences of interest, the chatter of the girls or some remark of Mrs. Wheeler's would drown the voices of the men in the room.

One time, indeed, he heard clearly: "When the Sycamore on the ridge goes into Massachusetts—" but this was sheer nonsense, and he concluded he must have misunderstood.

Later, they all forgathered in the living-room and there was music and general conversation.

Genevieve Lane proved herself decidedly entertaining, and though Samuel Appleby looked a little amusedly at his stenographer, he smiled kindly at her as he noticed that she in no way overstepped the bounds of correct demeanor.

Genevieve was thinking of what Keefe had said to her: "If you do only what is absolutely correct and say what is only absolutely correct, you can do whatever you like."

She had called it nonsense at the time, but she was beginning to see the truth of it. She was careful that her every word and act should be correct, and she was most decidedly doing as she liked. She made good with Mrs. Wheeler and Maida with no trouble at all; but she felt, vaguely, that Mr. Wheeler didn't like her. This she set about to remedy.

Going to his side, as he chanced to sit for a moment alone, she smiled ingratiatingly and said:

"I wonder if you can imagine, sir, what it means to me to see the inside of a house like this?"

"Bless my soul, what do you mean?" asked Wheeler, puzzled at the girl's manner.

"It's like a glimpse of Fairyland," she went on. "You see, I'm terribly ambitious—oh, fearfully so! And all my ambitions lead to just this sort of a home. Do you suppose I'll ever achieve it, Mr. Wheeler?"

Now the girl had truly wonderful magnetic charm, and even staid old Dan Wheeler was not insensible to the note of longing in her voice, the simple, honest admission of her hopes.

"Of course you will, little one," he returned, kindly. "I've heard that whatever one wants, one gets, provided the wish is strong enough." He spoke directly to her, but his gaze wandered as if his thoughts were far away.

"Do you really believe that?" Genevieve's big blue eyes begged an affirmation.

"I didn't say I believed it—I said I have heard it." He smiled sadly. "Not quite the same—so far as I'm concerned; but quite as assuring to you. Of course, my belief wouldn't endorse the possibility."

"It would for me," declared Genevieve. "I've lots of confidence in other people's opinions—"

"Anybody's?"

"Anybody whom I respect and believe in."

"Appleby, for instance?"

"Oh, yes, indeed! I'd trust Mr. Appleby's opinions on any subject. Let's go over there and tell him so."

Samuel Appleby was sitting at the other end, the north end of the long room. "No," said Wheeler, "I'm too comfortable here to move—ask him to come here."

Genevieve looked at him a little astonished. It was out of order, she thought, for a host to speak thus. She pressed the point, saying there was a picture at the other end of the room she wished to examine.

"Run along, then," said Wheeler, coolly. "Here, Maida, show Miss Lane that etching and tell her the interesting details about it."

The girls went away, and soon after Keefe drifted round to Wheeler's side.

"You know young Sam Appleby?" he asked, casually.

"No," Wheeler said, shortly but not sharply. "I daresay he's a most estimable chap."

"He's all of that. He's a true chip of the old block. Both good gubernatorial timber, as I'm sure you agree."

"What makes you so sure, Mr. Keefe?"

Curt Keefe looked straight at him. "Well," he laughed, "I'm quite ready to admit that the wish was father to the thought."

"Why do you call that an admission?"

"Oh," Keefe readily returned, "it is usually looked upon as a confession that one has no reason for a thought other than a wish."

"And why is it your wish?"

"Because it is the wish of my employer," said Keefe, seriously. "I know of no reason, Mr. Wheeler, why I shouldn't say that I hope and trust you will use your influence to further the cause of young Appleby."

"What makes you think I can do so?"

"While I am not entirely in Mr. Appleby's confidence, he has told me that the campaign would be greatly aided by your willingness to help, and so I can't help hoping you will exercise it."

"Appleby has told you so much, has he? No more?"

"No more, I think, regarding yourself, sir. I know, naturally, the details of the campaign so far as it is yet mapped out."

"And you know why I do not want to lend my aid?"

"I know you are not in accordance with the principles of the Appleby politics—"

"That I am not! Nor shall I ever be. Nor shall I ever pretend to be—"

"Pretend? Of course not. But could you not be persuaded?"

"By what means?"

"I don't know, Mr. Wheeler," and Keefe looked at him frankly. "I truly don't know by what means. But I do know that Mr. Appleby is here to present to you an argument by which he hopes to persuade you to help young Sam along—and I earnestly desire to add any word of mine that may help influence your decision. That is why I want to tell you of the good traits of Sam Appleby, junior. It may be I can give you a clearer light on his character than his father could do that is, I might present it as the opinion of a friend—"

"And not exaggerate his virtues as a father might do? I see. Well, Mr. Keefe, I appreciate your attitude, but let me tell you this: whatever I do or don't do regarding this coming campaign of young Appleby will be entirely irrespective of the character or personality of that young man. It will all depend on the senior Appleby's arrangements with me, and my ability to change his views on some of the more important planks in his platform. If he directed you to speak to me as you have done, you may return that to him as my answer."

"You, doubtless, said the same to him, sir?"

"Of course I did. I make no secret of my position in this matter. Samuel Appleby has a hold over me—I admit that—but it is not strong enough to make me forget my ideas of right and wrong to the public. No influence of a personal nature should weigh against any man's duty to the state, and I will never agree to pretend to any dissimulation in order to bring about a happier life for myself."

"But need you subscribe to the objectionable points to use your influence for young Sam?"

"Tacitly, of course. And I do not choose even to appear to agree to principles abhorrent to my sense of justice and honesty, thereby secretly gaining something for myself."

"Meaning your full pardon?"

Wheeler turned a look of surprise on the speaker.

"I thought you said you hadn't Appleby's full confidence," he said.

"Nor have I. I do know—as do many men—that you were pardoned with a condition, but the condition I do not know. It can't be very galling." And Keefe looked about on the pleasant surroundings.

"You think not? That's because you don't know the terms. And yet, galling though they are, hateful though it makes my life, and the lives of my wife and daughter, we would all rather bear it than to deviate one iota from the path of strict right."

"I must admire you for that, as must any honorable man. But are there not degrees or shadings of right and wrong—"

"Mr. Keefe, as an old man, I take the privilege of advising you for your own good. All through your life I beg you remember this: Anyone who admits degrees or shadings of right or wrong—is already wrong. Don't be offended; you didn't claim those things, you merely asked the question. But, remember what I said about it."

CHAPTER 3: ONE LAST ARGUMENT

Adjoining the bedroom of Samuel Appleby at Sycamore Ridge was a small sitting-room, also at his disposal. Here, later that same evening he sat in confab with his two assistants.

"We leave to-morrow afternoon," he said to Keefe and Miss Lane. "But before that, we've much to do. So far, we've accomplished nothing. I am a little discouraged but not disheartened. I still have a trump card to play, but I don't want to use it unless absolutely necessary."

"If you were inclined to take us further into your confidence, Mr. Appleby," Keefe began, and the older man interrupted :

"That's just what I propose to do. The time has come for it. Perhaps if you both know the situation you may work more intelligently."

"Sure we could!" exclaimed Genevieve. She was leaning forward in her chair, clasping her knees, her pretty evening frock disclosing her babyishly soft neck and arms; but without a trace of self-consciousness, she thought only of the subject they were discussing.

"There's something queer," she went on. "I can't see through it. Why does Mr. Wheeler act so polite most of the time, and then do some outrageous thing, like—"

"Like what?"

"Like refusing to cross the room—or—why, he declined point-blank to go with me to the north arbor, yet was perfectly willing to take me to the Japanese tea-house!"

"That's just the point of the whole thing," said Appleby, seriously; "here's the explanation in a nutshell. Years ago, Daniel Wheeler was pardoned for a crime he had committed—"

"He did commit it, then?" interrupted Keefe.

"He was tried and convicted. He was sentenced. And I, being governor at the time, pardoned him on the one condition, that he never again set foot inside the boundaries of the State of Massachusetts."

"Whee!" exclaimed Genevieve; "never go to Boston!"

"Nor anywhere else in the state. But this is the complication: Mrs. Wheeler, who is, by the way, a distant connection of my own family, inherited a large fortune on condition that she live in Massachusetts. So you see, the situation was peculiar. To keep her inheritance, Mrs. Wheeler must live in Massachusetts. Yet Mr. Wheeler could not enter the state without forfeiting his pardon."

"What a mess!" cried Genevieve, but Keefe said: "You planned that purposely, Mr. Appleby?"

"Of course," was the straightforward reply.

"Then I don't see how you can expect Mr. Wheeler's help in the campaign."

"By offering him a complete pardon, of course."

"But go on with the story," demanded Genevieve. "What did they do about the Massachusetts business?"

"As you see," returned Appleby, "this house is built on the state line between Massachusetts and Connecticut. It is carefully planned and built, and all the rooms or parts of rooms that Mr. Wheeler uses or enters are on the Connecticut side, yet the house is more than half in Massachusetts, which secures the estate to Mrs. Wheeler."

"Well, I never!" Genevieve exclaimed. "So that's why he can't go to the north arbor—it's in Massachusetts!"

"Of course it is. Also, he never goes into the northern end of the dining-room or the living-room."

"Or hall."

"Or hall. In fact, he merely is careful to keep on his own side of a definitely drawn line, and therefore complies with the restrictions. His den and his own bedroom and bath are all on the south side, while Mrs. Wheeler has a sitting-room, boudoir, and so forth, on the north side. She and Maida can go all over the house, but Mr. Wheeler is restricted. However, they've lived that way so long, it has become second nature to them, and nobody bothers much about it."

"Do people know?" asked Keefe. "The neighbors, I mean."

"Oh, yes; but, as I say, it makes little confusion. The trouble comes, as Miss Lane suggested, when Wheeler wants to go to Boston or anywhere in Massachusetts."

"Yet that is a small thing, compared with his freedom," observed Keefe; "I think he got off easy."

"But with Wheeler it isn't so much the deprivation as the stigma. He longs for a full pardon, and would do most anything to have it, but he refuses to stand for Sam's election, even with that for a bribe."

"You can't pardon him now that you aren't governor, can you, Mr. Appleby?" asked Genevieve.

"I can arrange to have it done. In fact, the present governor is ready and even anxious to pardon him, but I hold the key to that situation, myself. You two needn't know all the details, but now you know the principal points, and I expect you to utilize them."

"I'm willing enough," and Genevieve rocked back and forth thoughtfully, "and I may think of a way—but, for the moment, I don't."

"Get chummy with Maida," suggested Appleby.

"Let me do that," Keefe interrupted. "Without undue conceit, I believe I can influence the young lady, and I think Miss Lane, now that she knows the truth, can jolly up Mr. Wheeler to good effect."

"But, good gracious! What do you want to do?" and Genevieve giggled. "Say I entice the old gentleman over the line—then his pardon is canceled and he's a criminal—then you agree to ignore the lapse if he meets your wishes—is that the idea?"

Appleby smiled. "A little crude, Miss Lane. And beside, you couldn't get him over the line. He's too accustomed to his limitations to be caught napping, and not even your charms could decoy him over intentionally."

"Think so? Probably you're right. Well, suppose I try to work through Maida. If I could persuade Mr. Wheeler that she suffers from the stigma of her father's incomplete pardon—"

"Yes, that's it. This thing can't be accomplished by brutal threats, it must be done by subtle suggestion and convincing hints."

"That's my idea," agreed Keefe. "If I can talk straight goods to Miss Wheeler and make her see how much better it would be for her father in his latter years to be freed from all touch of the past disgrace, she might coax him to listen to you."

"That's right. Now, you know what you're here for; just do what you can—but don't make a mess of things. I'd rather you did nothing than to do some fool thing!"

"Trust us!" Genevieve encouraged him, as she rose. "Me and Curt may not put over a big deal, but we won't do anything silly."

The two men smiled as the girl, with a pleasant good-night, went away to her own room.

"She's true blue," said Keefe.

"Yes, she is," Appleby nodded. "All her frivolity is on the surface, like her powder and paint. At heart, that child has only my interests. I quite appreciate it."

"I hope you think the same of me, Mr. Appleby."

"I do, Keefe. More, I trust you with my most confidential matters. I'll own I want this business here to come out in my favor. I can't push Wheeler too hard—so I ask your help. But, as I hinted, I've one rod yet in pickle. If necessary, I'll use it, but I'd rather not."

"Of course I hope you won't have to, but, I'll admit I don't see much chance of succeeding with the present outlook."

"To-morrow morning will tell. If we can't work the thing through by noon, say—I'll spring my last trap. Good-night, Keefe."

"Good-night, Mr. Appleby."

Without apparent coercion the morning hours brought about a cozy session on the south veranda with Miss Lane and Daniel Wheeler in attendance, while at the same time, Keefe and Maida wandered over the beautiful park of the estate.

Keefe had gently guided the conversation into confidential channels, and when he ventured to sympathize with the girl in regard to her father's deprivation he was surprised at her ready acceptance of it.

"Oh, you know, don't you, Mr. Keefe!" she exclaimed. "But you don't know all it means to me. You see "—she blushed but went steadily on—" you see, I'm engaged to—to a man I adore. And—"

"Don't tell me if you'd rather not," he murmured.

"No, it's a relief to tell—and, somehow—you seem so wise and strong—"

"Go on then—please,"

The kind voice helped her and Maida resumed: "Well, Jeff—Mr. Allen, lives in Boston, and so..."

"So it would be very awkward if your father couldn't go there."

"Not only that—but I've made a vow never to step foot into Massachusetts until my father can do so, too. Nothing would induce me to break that vow!"

"Not even your lover?" said Keefe, astonished.

"No; my father is more to me than any lover."

"Then you don't truly love Mr. Allen."

"Oh, yes, I do—I do! But father is my idol. I don't believe any girl ever adored her father as I do. All my life I've had only the one object—to make him forget—as far as possible, his trouble. Now, if I were to marry and leave him—why, I simply couldn't do it!"

"Can't Mr. Allen live in Connecticut?"

"No; his business interests are all in Boston, and he can't be, transplanted. Oh, if father could only do what Mr. Appleby wants him to, then we could all be happy."

"Can't you persuade him?"

"I've tried my best. Mother has tried, too. But, you see, it's a matter of principle, and when principle is involved, we are all in the same boat. Mother and I would scorn any wrongdoing quite as much as father does."

"And you'll give up your life happiness for a principle?"

"Of course. Wouldn't you? Wouldn't every decent person? I couldn't live at all, if I were knowingly doing wrong."

"But your —" Keefe stopped abruptly.

"I know what you were going to say," Maida spoke sadly; "you were going to say my father did wrong. I don't believe he did."

"Don't you know?"

"I know in my own heart. I know he is incapable of the crime he was charged with. I'm sure he is shielding some one else, or else some one did it of whom he has no knowledge. But my father commit a crime? Never!"

"Do you care to tell me the details?"

"I don't know why I shouldn't. It was long ago, you know, and dad was accused of forgery. It was proved on him—or the jury thought it was—and he was convicted—"

"And sentenced?"

"Yes; to a long prison term. But Governor Appleby pardoned him with that mean old proviso, that he never should step into Massachusetts!"

"Was your mother then the heir to the Massachusetts property?"

"No; but Mr. Appleby knew she would be. So, when she did inherit, and had to live in Massachusetts to hold the estate, Mr. Appleby thought he had dad where he wanted him."

"Were they foes?"

"Politically, yes. Because dad did all he could to keep Mr. Appleby from being governor."

"But didn't succeed?"

"No; but almost. So, then, Mr. Appleby did this pardon trick to get even with father, and I think it turned out more serious than he anticipated. For mother took up the feud, and she got lawyers and all that and arranged to have the house built on the line between the states!"

"Was the estate she inherited on both sides of the line?"

"Oh, no; but it was near the southern border of Massachusetts, and she bought enough adjoining land to make the arrangement possible."

"Then the house isn't on the ground she inherited?"

"Not quite, but the lawyers decided it so that she really complies with the terms of the will, so it's all right."

"Was your mother the only heir?"

"So far as we can find out. I believe there was another branch of the family, but we haven't been able to trace it, so as the years go by, we feel more and more confident there's no other heir. Of course, should one turn up, his claim would be recognized."

Further talk quickly convinced Keefe that there was no hope of persuading Maida Wheeler to influence or advise her father in any direction other than his idea of right. No amount of urging or arguing would make Wheeler see his duty other than he now saw it, or make Maida endeavor to change his views. With a sigh over his failure, Keefe deftly turned the talk in other channels, and then they strolled back to the house.

As was to be expected, Genevieve had made no progress with her part of the plan. Her talk with Mr. Wheeler had availed nothing. He was courteous and kind; he was amused at her gay, merry little ways; he politely answered her questions, both serious and flippant, but absolutely nothing came of it all.

Samuel Appleby had a short but straightforward conversation with Mrs. Wheeler.

"Now, Sara," he said, "remember I'm your old friend as well as your relative."

"I don't call you a relative," she returned, calmly.

"A family connection, then; I don't care what you call it. And I'm going to speak right out, for I know better than to try sophistries. If you can get Dan to play my game regarding my son's campaign, I'll see that Dan gets full pardon, and at once. Then Maida can marry young Allen and you can all go to Boston to live."

"Sam Appleby, I'd rather never see Boston again, never have Dan see it, than to have him agree to endorse principles that he does not believe! And Dan feels the same way about it."

"But don't you consider your daughter? Will you condemn Maida to a broken-hearted life?"

"Maida must decide for herself. I think Jeffrey Allen will yet persuade her to leave her father. She is devoted to Dan, but she is deeply in love with Jeff and it's only natural she should go with him. Any other girl would do so without a second thought. Maida is unusual, but I doubt if she can hold out much longer against her lover's pleading."

"I think she will. Maida has your own unbreakable will."

"So be it, then. The child must choose for herself. But it doesn't alter the stand Dan and I have taken."

"Nothing can alter that?"

"Nothing, Samuel Appleby."

"That remains to be seen. Have I your permission to talk to Maida, alone?"

"Certainly. Why not? If you can persuade her to marry Jeff, I'll be only too glad. If you find her determined to stand by her father, then the case remains as it is at present."

And so, as Maida returned from her walk with Keefe, she was asked to go for another stroll with Samuel Appleby.

She assented, though with no show of pleasure at the prospect.

But as they started off, she said: "I'm glad to have a talk with you, Mr. Appleby. I want to appeal to your better nature."

"Good! That's just what I want—to appeal to yours. Suppose you word your appeal first."

"Mine is simple to understand. It is only that having had your way and having spoiled my father's life for fifteen years, I ask you, in the name of humanity and justice, to arrange matters so that his latter years of life shall be free from the curse you put upon him."

"I didn't put it upon him—he brought it on himself."

"He never committed that crime—and you know it!"

"What do you mean by that?" Appleby gave her a startled glance.

Had Maida seen this glance, she might have been enlightened. But her eyes were cast down, and she went on: "I don't know it surely, but I am positive in my own heart father never did it. However, that's past history. All I ask now is his full pardon—which, I know, you can bring about if you want to."

"And I will, willingly and gladly, if your father will grant my request."

"To put your son in as governor with the same political views that prevented my father from voting for you! You know he can't do that!"

"And yet you expect me to favor him!"

"But don't you see the difference? Your pardon will mean everything to father—"

"And to you!"

"Yes, but that's a secondary consideration. I'd ask this for father just the same, if it meant disaster for me!"

"I believe you would!" and Appleby gazed admiringly at the sweet, forceful face, and the earnest eyes.

"Of course I should! As I say, it means life's happiness to him."

"And his consent means just as much to me."

"No, it doesn't. That's just it. Even though father doesn't definitely help you in your son's election, he will do nothing to hinder. And that's much the same."

"It's far from being the same. His positive and definite help is a very different matter from his negative lack of interference. It's the help I want. And I do want it! Do you suppose I'd come here and urge it—beg for it—if I didn't think it absolutely necessary?"

"No; I suppose not. But I know he never will grant it, so you may as well give up hope."

"You know that, do you, Maida?" Appleby's voice was almost wistful.

"I most certainly do," and the girl nodded her head positively.

"Then listen to me. I have one argument yet unused. I'm going to use it now. And with you."

Maida looked up in alarm. Appleby's face was stern, his tone betokened a final, even desperate decision.

"Oh, not with me," she cried; "I—I'm only a girl—I don't know about these things—let's go where father is."

"No; you are the one. In your hands must rest your father's fate—your father's future. Sit here, beneath the old sycamore—you know about the tree?"

"Yes, of course."

"Never mind that now; I've only a few moments, but that's time enough. You know, Maida, how your mother holds this estate?"

"Yes—she must live in Massachusetts. Well, we do. The lawyers said—"

"That isn't the point; this is it. There is another heir."

"We've always thought it possible." Maida spoke coolly, though a dull fear clutched her heart.

"It's more than a possibility, it's a fact. I know it—and I know the heir."

"Who is it?"

"Never mind for the moment. Suffice it to say that he doesn't know it himself—that no one knows it but me.

Now, you and I know. No one else does. Do you understand?"

His keen gaze at her made her understand.

"I—" she faltered.

"You do understand," he asserted. "You sense my proposition before I make it. And you have it right— you're a smart girl, Maida, Yes, I suggest that you and I keep our secret, and that in return for my silence you persuade your father to meet my wishes. Then, he shall be fully pardoned, and all will be well."

"You criminal! You dishonest and dishonorable man!" she cried, her eyes blazing, her cheeks reddening with her righteous indignation,

"There, there, my girl, have a care. You haven't thought it all out yet. Doubtless you're going to say that neither your father nor mother want to remain here, if my statement is true."

"Of course I say that! They won't want to stay a minute! Who is the heir? Tell me!"

"And have you thought what it will mean to them to leave this place? Have you realized that your father has no business interests nor can he find any at his age? Do you remember that your mother has no funds outside the estate she inherited? Do you want to plunge them into penury, into pauperism, in their declining years?"

"Yes—if honesty requires it—" but the sweet voice trembled at the thought.

"Honesty is a good thing—a fine policy—but you are a devoted daughter, and I remind you that to tell this thing I have told you, means disaster—ruin for you and your parents. Young Allen can't support them—they are unaccustomed to deprivation—and," he lowered his voice, "this heir I speak of has no knowledge of the truth. He misses nothing, since he hopes for nothing."

Maida looked at him helplessly.

"I must think," she said, brokenly. "Oh, you are cruel, to put this responsibility on me."

"You know why I do it. I am not disinterested."

CHAPTER 4: THE BIG SYCAMORE TREE

At the south door the Appleby car stood waiting.

Genevieve was saying good-bye to Maida, with the affection of an old friend.

"We're coming back, you know," she reminded, "in two or three days, and please say you'll be glad to see me!"

"Of course," Maida assented, but her lip trembled and her eyes showed signs of ready tears.

"Cheer up," Genevieve babbled on. "I'm your friend—whatever comes with time!"

"So am I," put in Curtis Keefe. "Good-bye for a few days, Miss Wheeler."

How Maida did it, she scarcely knew herself, but she forced a smile, and even when Samuel Appleby gave her a warning glance at parting she bravely responded to his farewell words, and even gaily waved her hand as the car rolled down the drive.

Once out of earshot, Appleby broke out:

"I played my trump card! No, you needn't ask me what I was, for I don't propose to tell you. But it will take the trick, I'm sure. Why, it's got to!"

"It must be something pretty forcible, then," said Keefe, "for it looked to me about as likely as snow in summertime, that any of those rigid Puritans would ever give in an inch to your persuasions."

"Or mine," added Genevieve. "Never before have I failed so utterly to make any headway when I set out to be really persuasive."

"You did your best, Miss Lane," and Appleby looked at her with the air of one appraising the efficiency of a salesman. "I confess I didn't think Wheeler would be quite such a hardshell after all these years."

"He's just like concrete," Keefe observed. "They all are. I didn't know there were such conscientious people left in this wicked old world!"

"They're not really in the world," Appleby declared. "They've merely vegetated in that house of theirs, never going anywhere—"

"Oh, come now, Mr. Appleby," and Genevieve shook her head, "Boston isn't the only burg on the planet! They often go to New York, and that's going some!"

"Not really often—I asked Wheeler. He hasn't been, for five or six years, and though Maida goes occasionally, to visit friends, she soon runs back home to her father."

"It doesn't matter," Keefe said, "they're by no means mossbacks or hayseeds. They're right there with the goods, when it comes to modern literature or up-to-date news—"

"Oh, yes, they're a highbrow bunch," Appleby spoke impatiently; "but a recluse like that is no sort of a man! The truth is, I'm at the end of my patience! I've got to put this thing over with less palaver and circumlocution. I thought I'd give him a chance—just put the thing up to him squarely once—and, as he doesn't see fit to meet me half-way, he's got to be the loser, that's all."

"He seems to be the loser, as it is." This from Keefe.

"But nothing to what's coming to him! Why, the idea of my sparing him at all is ridiculous! If he doesn't come down, he's got to be wiped out! That's what it amounts to!"

"Wiped out—how?"

"Figuratively and literally! Mentally, morally and physically! That's how! I've stood all I can—I've waited long enough—too long—and now I'm going to play the game my own way! As I said, I played a trump card—I raised one pretty definite ruction just before we left. Now, that may do the business—and, it may not! If not, then desperate measures are necessary—and will be used!"

"Good gracious, Mr. Appleby!" Genevieve piped up from her fur collar which nearly muffled her little face. "You sound positively murderous!"

"Murder! Pooh, I'd kill Dan Wheeler in a minute, if that would help Sam! But I don't want Wheeler dead—I want him alive—I want his help—his influence—yet, when he sits there looking like a stone wall, and about as easy to overthrow, I declare I could kill him! But I don't intend to. It's far more likely he'd kill me!"

"Why?" exclaimed Keefe. "Why should he? And—but you're joking."

"Not at all. Wheeler isn't of the murderer type, or I'd be taking my life in my hands to go into his house! He hates me with all the strength of a hard, bigoted, but strictly just nature. He thinks I was unjust in the matter of his pardon, he thinks I was contemptible, and false to our old-time friendship; and he would be honestly and truly glad if I were dead. But—thank heaven—he's no murderer!"

"Of course not!" cried Genevieve. "How you do talk! As if murder were an everyday performance! Why, people in our class don't kill each other!"

The placid assumption of equality of class with her employer was so consistently Miss Lane's usual attitude, that it caused no mental comment from either of her hearers. Her services were so valuable that any such little idiosyncrasy was tolerated.

"Of course we don't—often," agreed Appleby, "but I'd wager a good bit that if Dan Wheeler could bump me off without his conscience knowing it—off I'd go!"

"I don't know about that," said Genevieve, musingly—"but I do believe that girl would do it!"

"What?" cried Keefe. "Maida!"

"Yes; she's a lamb for looks, but she's got a lion's heart—if anybody ever had one! Talk about a tigress protecting her cubs; it would be a milk-and-water performance beside Maida Wheeler shielding her father—or fighting for him—yes, or killing somebody for him!"

"Rubbish!" laughed Appleby. "Maida might be willing enough, in that lion heart of hers—but little girls don't go around killing people."

"I know it, and I don't expect her to. But I only say she's capable of it."

"Goethe says—(Keefe spoke in his superior way)—'We are all capable of crime, even the best of us.'"

"I remember that phrase," mused Appleby. "Is it Goethe's? Well, I don't say it's literally true, for lots of people are too much of a jellyfish makeup to have such a capability. But I do believe there are lots of strong, forcible people, who are absolutely capable of crime—if the opportunity offers."

"That's it," and Genevieve nodded her head wisely. "Opportunity is what counts. I've read detective stories, and they prove it. Be careful, Mr. Appleby, how you trust yourself alone with Mr. Wheeler."

"That will do," he reprimanded. "I can take care of myself, Miss Lane."

Genevieve always knew when she had gone too far, and, instead of sulking, she tactfully changed the subject and entertained the others with her amusing chatter, at which she was a success.

At that very moment, Maida Wheeler, alone in her room, was sobbing wildly, yet using every precaution that she shouldn't be heard.

Thrown across her bed, her face buried in the pillows, she fairly shook with the intensity of her grief.

But, as often happens, after she had brought her crying spell to a finish—and exhausted Nature insists on a finish—she rose and bathed her flushed face and sat down to think it out calmly.

Yet the more she thought the less calm she grew.

For the first time in her life she was face to face with a great question which she could not refer to her parents. Always she had confided in them, and matters that seemed great to her, even though trifling in themselves, were invariably settled and straightened out by her wise and loving father or mother.

But now, Samuel Appleby had told her a secret—a dreadful secret—that she must not only weigh and decide about, but must—at last, until she decided—keep from her parents.

"For," Maida thought, "if I tell them, they'll at once insist on knowing who the rightful heir is, they'll give over the place to him—and what will become of us?"

Her conscience was as active as ever it was, her sense of right and wrong was in no way warped or blunted, but instinct told her that she must keep this matter entirely to herself until she had come to her own conclusion. Moreover, she realized, the conclusion must be her own— the decision must be arrived at by herself, and unaided.

Finally, accepting all this, she resolved to put the whole thing out of her mind for the moment. Her parents were so intimately acquainted with her every mood or shade of demeanor, they would see at once that something was troubling her mind, unless she used the utmost care to prevent it Care, too, not to overdo her precaution. It would be quite as evident that she was concealing something, if she were unusually gay or carefree of manner.

So the poor child went downstairs, determined to forget utterly the news she had heard, until such time as she could be again by herself.

And she succeeded. Though haunted by a vague sense of being deceitful, she behaved so entirely as usual, that neither of her parents suspected her of pretense.

Moreover, the subject of Samuel Appleby's visit was such a fruitful source of conversation that there was less chance of minor considerations.

"Never will I consent," her father was reiterating, as Maida entered the room. "Why, Sara, I'd rather have the conditional pardon rescinded, rather pay full penalty of my conviction, than stand for the things young Sam's campaign must stand for!"

A clenched fist came down on the table by way of emphasis.

"Now, dad," said Maida, gaily, "don't thump around like that! You look as if you'd like to thump Mr. Appleby!"

"And I should! I wish I could bang into his head just how I feel about it—"

"Oh, he knows!" and Mrs. Wheeler smiled. "He knows perfectly how you feel."

"But, truly, mother, don't you think dad could—well, not do anything wrong—but just give in to Mr. Appleby—for—for my sake?"

"Maida—dear—that is our only stumbling-block. Your father and I would not budge one step, for ourselves—but for you, and for Jeffrey—oh, my dear little girl, that's what makes it so hard."

"For us, then—father, can't you—for our sake—"

Maida broke down. It wasn't for her sake she was pleading—nor for the sake of her lover. It was for the sake of her parents—that they might remain in comfort—and yet, comfort at the expense of honesty? Oh, the problem was too great—she hadn't worked it out yet.

"I can't think," her father's grave voice broke in on her tumultuous thoughts. "I can't believe, Maida, that you would want my freedom at the cost of my seared conscience."

"No, oh, no, father, I don't—you know I don't. But what is this dreadful thing you'd have to countenance if you linked up on the Appleby side? Are they pirates—or rascals?"

"Not from their own point of view," and Dan Wheeler smiled. "They think we are! You can't understand politics, child, but you must know that a man who is heart and soul in sympathy with the principles of his party can't conscientiously cross over and work for the other side."

"Yes, I know that, and I know that tells the whole story. But, father, think what there is at stake. Your freedom—and—ours!"

"I know that, Maida dear, and you can never know how my very soul is torn as I try to persuade myself that for those reasons it would be right for me to consent. Yet——"

He passed his hand wearily across his brow, and then folding his arms on the table he let his head sink down upon them.

Maida flew to his side. "Father, dearest," she crooned over him, as she caressed his bowed head, "don't think of it for a minute! You know I'd give up anything—I'd give up Jeff—if it means one speck of good for you."

"I know it, dear child, but—run away, now, Maida, leave me to myself."

Understanding, both Maida and her mother quietly left the room.

"I'm sorry, girlie dear, that you have to be involved in these scenes," Mrs. Wheeler said fondly, as the two went to the sitting-room.

"Don't be that way, mother. I'm part of the family, and I'm old enough to have a share and a voice in all these matters. But just think what it would mean, if father had his pardon! Look at this room, and think, he has never been in it! Never has seen the pictures—the view from the window, the general coziness of it all."

"I know, dear, but that's an old story. Your father is accustomed to living only in his own rooms—"

"And not to be able to go to the other end of the dining-room or living-room, if he chooses! It's outrageous!"

"Yes, Maida, I quite agree—but no more outrageous than it was last week—or last year."

"Yes, it is! It grows more outrageous every minute! Mother, what did that old will say? That you must live in Massachusetts?"

"Yes—you know that, dear."

"Of course I do. And if you lived elsewhere, what then?"

"I forfeit the inheritance."

"And what would become of it?"

"In default of any other heirs, it would go to the State of Massachusetts."

"And there are no other heirs?"

"What ails you, Maida? You know all this. No, there are no other heirs."

"You're sure?"

"As sure as we can be. Your father had every possible search made. There were advertisements kept in the papers for years, and able lawyers did all they could to find heirs if there were any. And, finding none, we were advised that there were none, and we could rest in undisturbed possession,"

"Suppose one should appear, what then?"

"Then, little girl, we'd give him the keys of the house, and walk out."

"Where would we walk to?"

"I've no idea. In fact, I can't imagine where we could walk to. But that, thank heaven, is not one of our troubles. Your father would indeed be desperately fixed if it were! You know, Maida, from a fine capable business man, he became a wreck, because of that unjust trial."

"Father never committed the forgery?"

"Of course not, dear."

"Who did?"

"We don't know. It was cleverly done, and the crime was purposely fastened on your father, because he was about to be made the rival candidate of Mr. Appleby, for governor.

"I know. And Mr. Appleby was at the bottom of it!"

"Your father doesn't admit that—"

"He must have been."

"Hush, Maida. These matters are not for you to judge. You know your father has done all he honestly could to be fully pardoned, or to discover the real criminal, and as he hasn't succeeded, you must rest content with the knowledge that there was no stone left unturned."

"But, mother, suppose Mr. Appleby has something more up his sleeve. Suppose he comes down on dad with some unexpected, some unforeseen blow that—"

"Maida, be quiet. Don't make me sorry that we have let you into our confidence as far as we have. These are matters above your head. Should such a thing as you hint occur, your father can deal with it."

"But I want to help—"

"And you can best do that by not trying to help! Your part is to divert your father, to lore him and cheer him and entertain him. You know this, and you know for you to undertake to advise er suggest is not only ridiculous but disastrous."

"All right, mother, I'll be good. I don't mean to be silly."

"You are, when you assume ability you don't possess." Mrs. Wheeler's loving smile robbed the words of any harsh effect. "Run along now, and see if dad won't go for a walk with you; and don't refer to anything unpleasant."

Maida went, and found Wheeler quite ready for a stroll.

"Which way?" he asked as they crossed the south veranda.

"Round the park, and bring up under the tree, and have tea there," dictated Maida, her heart already lighter as she obeyed her mother's dictum to avoid unpleasant subjects.

But as they walked on, and trivial talk seemed to pall, they naturally reverted to the discussion of their recent guests.

"Mr. Appleby is an old curmudgeon," Maida declared; "Mr. Keefe is nice and well-behaved; but the little Lane girl is a scream! I never saw any one so funny. Now she was quite a grand lady, and then she was a common little piece! But underneath it all she showed a lot of good sense and I'm sure in her work she has real ability."

"Appleby wouldn't keep her if she didn't have," her father rejoined; "but why do you call him a curmudgeon? He's very well-mannered."

"Oh, yes, he is. And to tell the truth, I'm not sure just what a curmudgeon is. But—he's it, anyway."

"I gather you don't especially admire my old friend."

"Friend! If he's a friend—give me enemies!"

"Fie, fie, Maida, what do you mean? Remember, he gave me my pardon."

"Yes, a high old pardon! Say, dad, tell me again exactly how he worded that letter about the tree."

"I've told you a dozen times! He didn't mean anything anyhow. He only said, that when the big sycamore tree went into Massachusetts I could go."

"What a crazy thing to say, wasn't it?"

"It was because we had been talking about the play of Macbeth. You remember, 'Till Birnam. Wood shall come to Dunsinane."

"Oh, yes, and then it did come—by a trick."

"Yes, the men came, carrying branches. We'd been talking about it, discussing some point, and then—it seemed clever, I suppose—to Appleby, and he wrote that about the sycamore."

"Meaning—never?"

"Meaning never."

"But Birnam Wood did go."

"Only by a trick, and that would not work in this case. Why, are you thinking of carrying a branch of sycamore into Massachusetts?"

Maida returned his smile as she answered: "I'd manage to carry the whole tree in, if it would do any good! But, I s'pose, old Puritan Father, you're too conscientious to take advantage of a trick?"

"Can't say, till I know the details of the game. But I doubt Appleby's being unable to see through your trick, and then—where are you?"

"That wouldn't matter. Trick or no trick, if the big sycamore went into Massachusetts, you could go. But I don't see any good plan for getting it in. And, too, Sycamore Ridge wouldn't be Sycamore Ridge without it. Don't you love the old tree, dad?"

"Of course, as I love every stick and stone about the place. It has been a real haven to me in my perturbed life."

"Suppose you had to leave it, daddy?"

"I think I'd die, dear. Unless, that is, we could go back home."

"Isn't this home?"

"It's the dearest spot on earth—outside my native state."

"There, there, dad, don't let's talk about it. We're here for keeps—"

"Heaven send we are, dearest! I couldn't face the loss of this place. What made you think of such a thing?"

"Oh, I'm thinking of all sorts of things to-day. But, father, while we're talking of moving—couldn't you—oh, couldn't you, bring yourself, somehow, to do what Mr. Appleby wants you to do? I don't know much about it—but father, darling, if you only could!"

"Maida, my little girl, don't think I haven't tried. Don't think I don't realize what it means to you and Jeff. I know—oh, I do know how it would simplify matters if I should go over to the Appleby side—and push Sam's campaign—as I could do it. I know that it would mean my full pardon, my return to my old home, my reunion with old scenes and associations. And more than that, it would mean the happiness of my only child—my daughter—and her chosen husband. And yet, Maida, as God is my judge, I am honest in my assertion that I can't so betray my honor and spend my remaining years a living lie. I can't do it, Maida—I can't."

And the calm, sorrowful countenance he turned to the girl was more positive and final than any further protestation could have been.

Chapter 5: The Bugle Sounded Taps

Although the portions of the house and grounds that were used by Wheeler included the most attractive spots, yet there were many forbidden places that were a real temptation to him.

An especial one was the flower-covered arbor that had so charmed Genevieve and another was the broad and beautiful north veranda. To be sure, the south piazza was equally attractive, but it was galling to be compelled to avoid any part of his own domain. However, the passing years had made the conditions a matter of habit and it was only occasionally that Wheeler's annoyance was poignant.

In fact, he and his wife bore the cross better than did Maida. She had never become reconciled to the unjust and arbitrary dictum of the conditional pardon. She lived in a constant fear lest her father should some day inadvertently and unintentionally step on the forbidden ground, and it should be reported. Indeed, knowing her father's quixotic honesty, she was by no means sure he wouldn't report it himself.

It had never occurred—probably never would occur, and yet, she often imagined some sudden emergency, such as a fire, or burglars, that might cause his impulsive invasion of the other side of the house.

In her anxiety she had spoken of this to Samuel Appleby when he was there. But he gave her no satisfaction. He merely replied: "A condition is a condition."

Curtis Keefe had tried to help her cause, by saying: "Surely a case of danger would prove an exception to the rule," but Appleby had only shaken his head in denial.

Though care had been taken to have the larger part of the house on the Massachusetts side of the line, yet the rooms most used by the family were in Connecticut. Here was Mr. Wheeler's den, and this had come to be the most used room in the whole house. Mrs. Wheeler's sitting-room, which her husband never had entered, was also attractive, but both mother and daughter invaded the den, whenever leisure hours were to be enjoyed.

The den contained a large south bay window, which was Maida's favorite spot. It had a broad, comfortable window-seat, and here she spent much of her time, curled up among the cushions, reading. There were long curtains, which, half-drawn, hid her from view, and often she was there for hours, without her father's knowing it.

His own work was engrossing. Cut off from his established law business in Massachusetts, he had at first felt unable to start it anew in different surroundings. Then, owing to his wife's large fortune, it was decided that he should give up all business for a time. And as the time went on, and there was no real necessity for an added income, Wheeler had indulged in his hobby of book collecting, and had amassed a library of unique charm as well as goodly intrinsic value.

Moreover, it kept him interested and occupied, and prevented his becoming morose or melancholy over his restricted life.

So, many long days he worked away at his books, and Maida, hidden in the window-seat, watched him lovingly in the intervals of her reading.

Sitting there, the morning after Samuel Appleby's departure, she read not at all, although a book lay open on her lap. She was trying to decide a big matter, trying to solve a vexed question.

Maida's was a straightforward nature. She never deceived herself. If she did anything against her better judgment, even against her conscience, it was with open eyes and understanding mind. She used no sophistry, no pretence, and if she acted mistakenly she was always satisfied to abide by the consequences.

And now, she set about her problem, systematically and methodically, determined to decide upon her course, and then strictly follow it.

She glanced at her father, absorbed in his book catalogues and indexes, and a great wave of love and devotion filled her heart. Surely no sacrifice was too great that would bring peace or pleasure to that martyred spirit.

That he was a martyr, Maida was as sure as she was that she was alive. She knew him too well to believe for an instant that he had committed a criminal act; it was an impossibility for one of his character. But that she could do nothing about. The question had been raised and settled when she was too young to know anything about it, and now, her simple duty was to do anything she might to ease his burden and to help him to forget.

"And," she said to herself, "first of all, he must stay in this home. He positively must—and that's all there is about that. Now, if he knows—if he has the least hint that there is another heir, he'll get out at once—or at least, he'll move heaven and earth to find the heir, and then we'll have to move. And where to? That's an unanswerable question. Anyway, I've only one sure conviction. I've got to keep from him all knowledge or suspicion of that other heir!

"Maybe it isn't true—maybe Mr. Appleby made it up—but I don't think so. At any rate, I have to proceed as if it were true, and do my best. And, first of all, I've got to hush up my own conscience. I've too much of my father's nature to want to live here if it rightfully belongs to somebody else. I feel like a thief already. But I'm going to bear that—I'm going to live under that horrid conviction that I'm living a lie—for father's sake."

Maida was in earnest. By nature and by training her conscience was acutely sensitive to the finest shades of right and wrong. She actually longed to announce the possibility of another heir and let justice decide the case. But her filial devotion was, in this thing, greater even than her conscience. Her mother, too, she knew, would be crushed by the revelation of the secret, but would insist on thorough investigation, and, if need be, on renunciation of the dear home.

Her mental struggle went on. At times it seemed as if she couldn't live beneath the weight of such a secret. Then, she knew she must do it. What was her own peace of mind compared with her father's? What was her own freedom of conscience compared with his tranquillity?

She thought of telling Jeffrey Allen. But, she argued, he would feel as the others would—indeed, as she herself did—that the matter must be dragged out into the open and settled one way or the other.

No; she must bear the brunt of the thing alone. She must never tell any one.

Then, the next point was, would Mr. Appleby tell? He hadn't said so, but she felt sure he would. Well, she must do all she could to prevent that. He was to return in a day or two. By that time she must work out some plan, must think up some way, to persuade him not to tell. What the argument would be, she had no idea, but she was determined to try her uttermost.

There was one way—but Maida blushed even at the thought.

Sam Appleby—young Sam—wanted to marry her— had wanted to for a year or more. Many times she had refused him, and many times he had returned for another attempt at persuasion. To consent to this would enable her to control the senior Appleby's revelations.

It would indeed be a last resort—she wouldn't even think of it yet; surely there was some other way!

The poor, tortured child was roused from her desperate plannings by a cheery voice, calling:

"Maida—Maida! Here's me!"

"Jeffrey!" she cried, springing from the window-seat, and out to greet him.

"Dear!" he said, as he took her in his arms. "Dear, dearer, dearest! What is troubling you?"

"Trouble? Nothing! How can I be troubled when you're here?"

"But you are! You can't fool me, you know! Never mind, you can tell me later. I've got three whole days—how's that?"

"Splendid! How did it happen?"

"Old Bennett went off for a week's rest—doctor's orders—and he said, if I did up my chores, nice and proper, I could take a little vacation myself. Oh, you peach! You're twice as beauti-fuller as ever!"

A whirlwind embrace followed this speech and left Maida, breathless and laughing, while her father smiled benignly upon the pair.

It was some hours later that, as they sat under the big sycamore, Jeffrey Allen begged Maida to tell him her troubles.

"For I know you're pretty well broken up over something," he declared.

"How do you know?" she smiled at him.

"Why, my girl, I know every shadow that crosses your dear heart."

"Do I wear my heart on my sleeve, then?"

"You don't have to, for me to see it. I recognize the signs from your face, your manner, your voice—your whole being is trembling with some fear or some deeply-rooted grief. So tell me all about it."

And Maida told. Not the last horrible threat that Samuel Appleby had told her alone, but the state of things as Appleby had presented it to Daniel Wheeler himself.

"And so you see, Jeff, it's, a deadlock. Father won't vote for young Sam—I don't mean only vote, but throw all his influence—and that means a lot—on Sam's side. And if he doesn't, Mr. Appleby won't get him pardoned—you know we hoped he would this year—"

"Yes, dear; it would mean so much to us."

"Yes, and to dad and mother, too. Well, there's no hope of that, unless father throws himself heart and soul into the Appleby campaign."

"And he won't do that?"

"Of course not. He couldn't, Jeff. He'd have to subscribe to what he doesn't believe in—practically subscribe to a lie. And you know father—"

"Yes, and you, too—and myself! None of us would want him to do that, Maida!"

"Doesn't necessity ever justify a fraud, Jeff?" The question was put so wistfully that the young man smiled.

"Nixy! and you know that even better than I do, dear. Why, Maida, what I love you most for—yes, even more than your dear, sweet, beauty of face, is the marvellous beauty of your nature, your character. Your flawless soul attracted me first of all—even as I saw it shining through your clear, honest eyes.'

"Oh, Jeffrey," and Maida's clear eyes filled with tears, "I'm not honest, I'm not true blue!"

"Then nobody on this green earth is! Don't say such things, dear. I know what you mean, that you think you want your father to sacrifice his principles, in part, at least, to gain his full pardon thereby. See how I read your thoughts! But, you don't really think that; you only think you think it. If the thing came to a focus, you'd be the first one to forbid the slightest deviation from the line of strictest truth and honor!"

"Oh, Jeff, do you think I would?"

"Of course I think so—I know it! You are a strange make-up, Maida. On an impulse, I can imagine you doing something wrong—even, something pretty awful—but with even a little time for thought you couldn't do a wrong."

"What!" Maida was truly surprised; "I could jump into any sort of wickedness?"

"I didn't quite put it that way," Jeff laughed, "but— well, you know it's my theory, that given opportunity, anybody can yield to temptation."

"Nonsense! It's a poor sort of honor that gives out at a critical moment!"

"Not at all. Most people can resist anything—except temptation! Given a strong enough temptation and a perfect opportunity, and your staunchest, most conscientious spirit is going to succumb."

"I don't believe that."

"You don't have to—and maybe it isn't always true. But it often is. Howsomever, it has no bearing on the present case. Your father is not going to lose his head—and though you might do so"—he smiled at her—"I can't see you getting a chance! You're not in on the deal, in any way, are you?"

"No; except that Mr. Appleby asked me to use all my influence with father."

"Which you've done?"

"Yes; but it made not the slightest impression."

"Of course not. I say, Maid, young Sam isn't coming down here, is he?"

"Not that I know of," but Maida couldn't help her rising color, for she knew what Allen was thinking.

"Just let him try it, that's all! Just let him show his rubicund countenance in these parts—if he wants trouble!"

"Does anybody ever want trouble?" Maida smiled a little.

"Why, of course they do! Sometimes they want it so much that they borrow it!"

"I'm not doing that! I've had it offered to me—in full measure, heaped up, pressed down, and running over."

"Poor little girl. Don't take it so hard, dearest. I'll have a talk with your father, and we'll see how matters really stand. I doubt it's as bad as you fear—and anyway, if no good results come our way, things are no worse than they have been for years. Your father has lived fairly contented and happy. Let things drift, and in another year or two, after the election is a thing of the past, we can pick up the pardon question again. By that time you and I will be—where will we be, Maida?"

"I don't know, Jeff—"

"Well, we'll be together, anyway. You'll be my wife, and if we can't live in Boston—we can live out of Boston! And that's all there is about that!"

"You'll have to come here to live. There's enough for us all."

"Settle down here and sponge on your mother! I see it! But, never you mind, lady fair, something will happen to smooth out our path. Perhaps this old tree will take it into its head to go over into Massachusetts, and so blaze a trail for your father—and you."

"Oh, very likely. But I've renewed my vow, Jeff; unless father can go into the state, I never will!"

"All right, sweetheart. Renew your vow whenever its time limit expires. I'm going to fix things so no vows will be needed—except our marriage vows. Will you take them, dear?"

"When the time comes, yes." But Maida did not smile, and Jeff, watching her closely, concluded there was yet some point on which she had not enlightened him. However, he asked no further question, but bided his time.

"Guess I'll chop down the old tree while I'm here, and ship it into Massachusetts as firewood," he suggested.

"Fine idea," Maida acquiesced, "but you'd only have your trouble for your pains. You see, the stipulation was, 'without the intervention of human hands.'—"

"All right, we'll chop it down by machinery, then."

"I wish the tree promise meant anything, but it doesn't. It was only made as a proof positive how impossible was any chance of pardon."

"But now a chance of pardon has come."

"Yes, but a chance that cannot be taken. You'll be here, Jeff, when they come back. Then you can talk with Mr. Appleby, and maybe, as man to man, you can convince him—"

"Convince nothing! Don't you suppose I've tried every argument I know of, with that old dunderhead? I've spent hours with him discussing your father's case. I've talked myself deaf, dumb and blind, with no scrap of success. But, I don't mind telling you, Maida, that I might have moved the old duffer to leniency if it hadn't been for—you."

"Me?"

"Yes; you know well enough young Sam's attitude toward you. And old Appleby as good as said if I'd give up my claim on your favor, and give sonny Sam a chance, there'd be hope for your father."

"H'm. Indeed! You don't say so! And you replied?"

"I didn't reply much of anything. For if I'd said what I wanted to say, he would have been quite justified in thinking that I was no fit mate for a Christian girl! Let's don't talk about it."

That night Maida went to her room, leaving Allen to have a long serious talk with her father.

She hoped much from the confab, for Jeff Allen was a man of ideas, and of good, sound judgment. He could see straight, and could advise sensibly and well. And Maida hoped, too, that something would happen or some way be devised that the secret told her by Appleby might be of no moment. Perhaps there was no heir, save in the old man's imagination. Or perhaps it was only someone who would inherit a portion of the property, leaving enough for their own support and comfort.

At any rate, she went to bed comforted and cheered by the knowledge that Jeff was there, and that if there was anything to be done he would do it.

She had vague misgivings because she had not told him what Appleby had threatened. But, she argued, if she decided to suppress that bit of news, she must not breathe it to anybody—not even Jeff.

So, encouraged at the outlook, and exhausted by her day of worriment, she slept soundly till well into the night.

Then she was awakened by a strange sound. It gave her, at first, a strange impression of being on an ocean steamer. She couldn't think why, for her half- awake senses responded only to the vague sense of familiarity with such a sound.

But wide awake in a moment, she heard more of it, and realized that it was a bugle to which she listened— the clear, though not loud, notes of a bugle. Amazed, she jumped from her bed, and looked out of a window in the direction of the sound.

She saw nothing, and heard the last faint notes die away, as she listened.

There was no further sound, and she returned to bed, and after a time fell asleep again.

She pondered over the occurrence while dressing next morning, wondering what it meant.

Downstairs she found only Jeffrey in the dining-room.

"Hear anything funny in the night, Maida?" he asked her.

"Yes; a bugle," she returned. "Did you hear it?"

"Of course I did. Who plays the thing around here?"

"No one, that I know of. Wasn't it rather strange?"

"Rath-er! I should say so. Made me think of the old English castles, where spooks walk the parapets and play on bugles or bagpipes or some such doings."

"Oh, those silly stories! But this was a real bugle, played by a real man."

"How do you know?"

"By the sound."

"Spook bugles sound just the same."

"How do you know?"

"How could they be heard if they didn't? Here's your father. Good-morning, Mr. Wheeler. Who's your musical neighbor?"

But Daniel Wheeler did not smile,

"Go up to your mother, Maida, dear," he said; "she— she isn't well. Cheer her up all you can."

"What's the trouble?" Allen asked, solicitously, as Maida ran from the room.

"A strange thing, my boy. Did you hear a bugle call last night?"

"Yes, sir; it sounded 'taps.' Is there a camp near by?"

"No; nothing of the sort. Now—well, to put it frankly, there is an old tradition in Mrs. Wheeler's family that a phantom bugler, in that very way, announces an approaching death."

"Good Lord! You don't mean she believes that!"

"She does, and what can I say to disprove her belief? We all heard it. Who could have done such a trick?"

"I don't know who, but somebody did. That bugle was played by a pair of good, strong human lungs—not by a spirit breath!"

"It sounded so, but that doesn't affect Mrs. Wheeler's belief. If I could produce the bugler, and get him to admit it, she might believe him, but otherwise, she's sure it was the traditional bugler, and that earthly days are numbered for some one of our little family."

"You don't believe this foolishness, sir?"

"I can't; my nature rejects the very idea of the supernatural. Yet, who could or would do it? There's no neighbor who would, and I know of no one round here who knows of the tradition."

"Oh, pshaw, it's the merest casual occurrence. A Boy Scout, like as not—or a gay young chap returning from a merry party. There are lots of explanations, quite apart from spooks!"

"I hope you can persuade Mrs. Wheeler of that. She is nervously ill, and will hear of no rational explanation for the bugle call."

"Beg her to come down to breakfast, do; then we'll all jolly her up until she loses her fears."

But though Allen's attempt was a brave one and ably seconded by Mrs. Wheeler's husband and daughter, they made not the slightest progress toward relieving her fears or disabusing her mind of her conviction.

CHAPTER 6: THE OTHER HEIR

A General air of vague foreboding hung over the
Wheeler household. Mrs. Wheeler tried to rally from the
shock of the inexplicable bugle call, but though she was
bright and cheerful, it was fully evident that her manner
was forced and her gayety assumed.

Maida, solicitous for her mother, was more than ever
resolved not to disclose the news of another possible heir
to the estate, though the more she thought about it, the
more she felt sure Samuel Appleby had spoken the truth.

She decided that he had learned of the other heir, and
that he was none too honest to be willing to keep the fact
a secret, if, in turn, he could serve his own ends. She did
not need to be told that if she would look on young Sam
with favor, her father would perforce lend his aid to the
campaign. And, in that case, she knew that the other heir
would never be mentioned again.

And yet, the price—the acceptance of young Sam, was
more than she could pay. To give up Jeff Allen, her own
true love, and marry a man of such a different type and
calibre as Sam Appleby was—it was too much! And Jeff
would have something to say about that! Yet, she must
decide for herself. If she made the supreme sacrifice, it
must be done as if of her own volition. If her parents or
her lover guessed that she was acting under compulsion,
they would put an end to the project.

But could she, even if willing to sacrifice herself, could
she ask Sam Appleby to take her? Yet she knew this
would be the easiest thing in the world. A mere hint to
Mr. Appleby that she approved of his son would bring the
younger man down to the house at once and matters
would then take care of themselves.

But could she do it? She looked at Jeff, as he sat talking to her father, his strong, fine face alight with the earnestness of their discussion. He was a man of a thousand—her own Jeffrey. No, she could not break his heart—she had no right to do that. It would be a crime to blot out the joy and happiness from the eager young face.

And then she looked at the other dear face. Her father, worn and aging, but still in rugged health. Could she let the inevitable happen, and see him turned out of the home that he loved—the home that had so long been his sanctuary, his refuge from the cold injustice of his fellow-men?

And her mother, almost ill from her fright and foreboding. To add the disaster of poverty and homelessness—no, she couldn't do that!

And so poor Maida wondered and worried; her thoughts going round in a circle, and coming back to the two men she loved, and knew she must break one heart or the other.

At one moment her duty to her parents seemed preeminent. Then, again, she realized a duty to herself and to the man who loved her.

"I don't know what to do," she thought, piteously; "I'll wait till Mr. Appleby comes back here, and then I'll tell him just how I'm placed. Perhaps I can appeal to his better nature."

But Maida Wheeler well knew that however she might appeal to Samuel Appleby, it would be in vain. She knew from the very fact that he came to her home, and made the offers and threats that he did make, that his mind was made up, and no power on earth could move him from his decision. He had a strong case, he probably thought; the offer of full pardon to Dan Wheeler, and the offer to Maida to keep quiet about another heir, would, he doubtless thought, be sufficient to win his cause.

"What an awful man he is," she thought. "I wish he were dead! I know I oughtn't to wish that, but I do. I'd kill him myself if it would help father. I oughtn't to say that—

and I don't suppose I really would do it, but it would simplify matters a lot! And somebody said, 'We are all capable of crime—even the best of us.' Well, of course I wouldn't kill the old man, but he'd better not give me a real good chance!"

"What are you thinking about, little girl?" asked Allen, turning to her.

Maida looked at him and then at her father, and said, deliberately:

"I was just thinking how I'd like to kill Samuel Appleby."

"Senior, junior, or both?" laughed Allen, who thought little of her words, save as a jest.

"Senior, I meant, but we may as well make it a wholesale slaughter."

"Don't, Maida," her father looked grieved. "Don't speak flippantly of such subjects."

"Well, father, why not be honest? Wouldn't you like to kill him?"

"No, child—not that."

"But you'd be glad if he were dead! There, you needn't answer. But if you were absolutely honest, you'd have to admit it."

"I'll admit it," said her mother, wearily. "Samuel Appleby has spoiled all our lives;—is still spoiling them. He does it for his own selfish interests. He has ruined the happiness of my husband, myself, my daughter, and my prospective son-in-law. Is it any wonder that we should honestly wish he were dead? It may not sound Christian—but it is an honest expression of human nature:"

"It is, Mrs. Wheeler," and Allen's face looked more pained than shocked. "But, all the same, we oughtn't to talk like that."

"No, indeed," agreed Wheeler. "Please, Maida, darling, don't say such things. And, Sara, if you must say them, say them to me when we are alone. It's no sort of talk for these young people's ears."

"Why, I said it before mother did!" Maida broke out. "And I mean it! I'm at the end of my rope. If that man is to hound us and torture us all our lives, I can't help wishing him dead."

"There, there, daughter, please don't."

"I won't, dad. I'll never say it again. But I put myself on record, and if the rest of you were honest, you'd do the same thing!"

"That we'd like to kill him?" asked Allen, smiling at the idea.

"I didn't say that—I said we wish him dead. If a nice, convenient stroke of lightning came his way, or—"

"Maida, hush!" her father spoke sternly; "I won't allow such talk! It isn't like you, my child, and it isn't—"

"Isn't good form, I s'pose!" she interrupted. "Well, I'll let up, dads, and I am a little ashamed of myself. Mother, maybe the phantom bugler was announcing the death of old Appleby!"

"Hush, Maida! What has got into you?"

"I'm incorrigible, I guess—"

"You are!" and Allen smiled fondly at her. "Come out for a walk in the sunshine with me, and get these awful thoughts out of your brain."

"I know I'm a criminal," said Maida, as they walked down a garden path; "but I can't help it. I've more to bear than you know of, Jeff, and you must make allowance."

"I do, sweetheart. And I know how you're troubled, and all that, but don't say such dreadful things. I know you don't mean them."

"No, I don't—at least, I don't think I do. But I won't say them any more. I think I lost my head—"

"Forget it. You're upset and nervous and your mother's worry reflects itself on you. Is there really a bugler tradition?"

"Not over here. There was one connected with mother's family long ago, in England, I believe. Of course, it was just one of those old spook yarns that most old houses have over there. But mother always remembered it. She has told everybody who ever visited here about it, and I think she always expected to hear the thing. Queer, though, wasn't it?"

"Not very. It's explainable by natural means, of course. Probably we'll never know who it was, but it was no phantom, be sure of that."

"Oh, well, it doesn't matter, except that it has upset mother so dreadfully. But she'll get over it—if nothing happens."

"Nothing will happen—if by that you mean a death in the family. More likely a marriage will take place!"

"Not ours, Jeff. I think that bugler sounded the death-knell of our hopes."

"Maida! What is the matter with you? Why are you talking like that? I know you've something on your mind that you haven't told me yet. Something pretty serious, for it makes you say the strangest things! Tell me, darling, won't you?"

"I can't, Jeff. I mean, there isn't anything. Wait till those people come back again. You'll be here, won't you? They're coming to-morrow."

"You bet I will! I'll see what I can do with old curmudgeon. You know I'm argumentative."

"That won't do any good with Appleby. What he wants is help from dad. If he doesn't get that, he'll punish us all."

"And he can't get that, for your dad won't give it. So it looks as if we must all take our punishment. Well, we're prepared."

"You wouldn't speak so lightly if you knew everything!"

"That's why I ask you to tell me everything. Do, Maida, I'm sure I can help you."

"Wait till they come," was all Maida would say in response to his repeated requests.

And at last they came.

Smiling and hearty, Samuel Appleby reentered the Wheeler home, apparently as self-assured and hopeful as when he left it.

Keefe was courteous and polite as always and Genevieve Lane was prettier than ever by reason of some new Boston-bought clothes.

Allen was introduced to the newcomers and sized up by one glance of Samuel Appleby's keen eyes. Privately he decided that this young man was a very formidable rival of his son. But he greeted Allen with great cordiality, which Jeff thought it best to return, although he felt an instinctive dislike for the man's personality.

"Come along with me, Maida," and with daring familiarity, Genevieve put her hand through Maida's arm and drew her toward the stairs. "I have the same room, I s'pose," she babbled on; "I've lots of new things I want to show you. And," she added as they entered the room, and she closed the door, "I want a talkfest with you before the others begin."

"What about?" asked Maida, feeling the subject would be one of importance.

"Well, it's just this. And don't be too shocked if I speak right out in meetin'. I've determined to marry into this bunch that I'm working for."

"Have you?" laughed Maida. "Are they equally determined?"

"I'm not joking—I'm in dead earnest. A poor girl has got to do the best she can for herself in this cold world. Well, I'm going to corral one of the three: old man Appleby, young man Appleby, or Curt Keefe."

"Which one, for choice?" Mai da still spoke lightly.

"You don't think I'm in earnest, but I am. Well, I'd rather have young Sam. Next, I'd choose his father; and, lastly, I'm pretty sure I could nail Curtis Keefe."

Maida couldn't help her disapproval showing in her face, but she said: "It isn't just the way I'd go about selecting a husband, but if it's your way, all right. Can I help you?"

"Do you mean that?"

"Why, yes, if I can do anything practical."

"Oh, you can! It's only to keep off the grass, regarding young Sam."

"You mean not to try to charm him myself?"

"Just about that. And I'll tell you why I say this. It seems old Appleby has about made up his mind that you're the right and proper mate for young Appleby. Oh, you needn't draw yourself up in that haughty fashion— he's good enough for you, Miss!"

"I didn't say he wasn't," and Maida laughed in spite of herself at Genevieve's manner. "But, truly, I don't want him. You see I'm engaged to Mr. Allen."

"I know it, but that cuts no ice with Pa Appleby. He plans to oust Mr. Allen and put his son in his place."

"Oh, he does, does he?" Maida's heart sank, for she had anticipated something like this. "Am I to be consulted?"

"Now, look here, Maida Wheeler. You needn't take that attitude, for it won't get you anywhere. You don't know Mr. Appleby as I do. What he says goes—goes, understand?"

Maida went white. "But such a thing as you speak of won't go!" she exclaimed.

"I'm not sure it won't, if he so ordains it," Miss Lane said, gravely. "But I just wanted your assurance that you don't hanker after Sammy-boy, so I can go ahead and annex him myself."

"In defiance of Mr. Appleby's intents?"

"I may be able to circumvent him. I'm some little schemer myself. And he may die."

"What?"

"Yep. He has an unsatisfactory heart, and it may go back on him at any minute."

"What a thing to bank on!"

"It may happen all the same. But I've other irons in the fire. Run along, now; I've work to do. You're a dear girl, Maida, and the time may come when I can help you."

The round, rosy-cheeked face looked very serious, and Maida said, gratefully: "I may be very glad of such help, Genevieve."

Then she went away.

Samuel Appleby was lying in wait for her.

"Here you are, my girl," he said, as she came downstairs. "Come for a ramble with me, won't you?"

And, knowing that the encounter was inevitable, Maida went.

Appleby wasted no time in preliminaries. "I've got to go home to-morrow morning," he said. "I've got to have this matter of your father's help in the campaign settled before I go."

"I thought it was settled," returned Maida, calmly. "You know he will never give you the help you ask. And oh, please, Mr. Appleby, won't you give up the question? You have ruined my father's life—all our lives; won't you cease bothering him, and, whether you let him get his full pardon or not, won't you stop trying to coerce his will?"

"No; I will not. You are very pleading and persuasive, my girl, but I have my own ax to grind. Now, here's a proposition. If you—I'll speak plainly—if you will consent to marry my son, I'll get your father's full pardon, and I'll not ask for his campaign support."

Maida gasped. All her troubles removed at once—but at such a price! She thought of Allen, and a great wave of love surged over her.

"Oh, I can't—I can't," she moaned. "What are you, Mr. Appleby? I love my chosen mate, my fiance, Jeffrey Allen. Would you ask me to give him up and marry your son, whom I esteem highly, but do not love?"

"Certainly; I ask just that. You are free to say yes or no!"

"Then, I say no. There must be some other way! Give me some other chance, even though it be a harder one!"

"All right, I will." Mr. Appleby's face was hard now, his lips set in a straight line; he was about to play his last card. "All right, I will. Here it is. The other heir, of whom I spoke to you the other day, is Curtis Keefe."

"Mr. Keefe!"

"Yes—but wait—he doesn't know it. I hit upon a clue in his chance reference to his mother's family, and unknown to him I investigated genealogies and all that, and it is positive, he is the heir to all this estate, and not your mother."

"You're sure?"

"Yes, absolutely certain. But, remember, he doesn't know it. He has no idea of such a thing. Now, if you'll marry Sam, Keefe shall never know. I'll burn all the papers that I have in evidence. You and I will forget the secret, and your father and mother can rest in undisturbed possession here for the rest of their lives."

"And you wouldn't insist on father's campaign work?"

"If you marry my son, I rather think your father will lend his aid—at least in some few matters, without urging. But he shall not be urged beyond his wishes, rest assured of that. In a word, Maida, all that you want or desire shall be yours except your choice of a husband. And I'll wager that inside of a year, you'll be wondering what you ever saw in young Allen, and rejoicing that you are the wife of the governor instead!"

"I can't do it—oh, I can't! And, then, too, there's Mr. Keefe—and the heirship!"

"Mr. Keefe and the airship!" exclaimed Curtis Keefe himself, as he came round the corner and met them face to face. "Am I to go up in an airship? And when?"

Appleby flashed a quick glance at Maida, which she rightly interpreted to mean to let Keefe rest unenlightened as to his error.

"You're not the Mr. Keefe we meant," said Appleby, smiling at his secretary. "There are others."

And then Appleby walked away, feeling his best plan was to let Maida think things over.

"What Keefe is going up in an airship?" Curt insisted, his curiosity aroused.

"I don't know," said Maida, listlessly. "Mr. Appleby was telling me some airship yarn. I didn't half listen. I—I can't bear that man!"

"I can't blame you for that, Miss Wheeler. But we're going away to-morrow, and he'll be out of your way."

"No; he has me in a trap. He has arranged it so—oh, what am I saying!"

"Don't go on, if you feel you might regret it. Of course, as Mr. Appleby's confidential secretary, I know most of his affairs. May I say that I'm very sorry for you, and may I offer my help, if you can use me in any way?"

"How kind you are, Mr. Keefe. But if you know the details of the matter, you know that I am in a fearful dilemma. Oh, if only that man were out of existence!"

"Oh, Miss Wheeler," and Keefe looked undisguisedly shocked.

"I don't mean anything wrong," Maida's eyes were piteous, "but I don't know what to do! I've no one to confide in—no way to turn for help—for advice—"

"Why, Miss Wheeler, you have parents, friends—"

"No one that I can speak to! Forgive me, Mr. Keefe, but I am nearly out of my mind. Forgive me, if I ask you to leave me—will you?"

"Of course, you poor child! I ought to have sensed that I was intruding!"

With a courteous bow, he walked away, leaving Maida alone on the seat beneath the old sycamore.

She thought long and deeply. She seemed to grow older and more matured of judgment as she dealt with the big questions in her mind.

After a long time she came to her decision. Torn and wracked with emotions, she bravely faced the many-sided situation, and made up her mind. Then she got up and walked into the house.

That afternoon, about five o'clock, Appleby and Wheeler sat in the latter's den, talking over the same old subject. Maida, hidden in the window-seat, was listening. They did not know she was there, but they would not have cared. They talked of nothing she did not already know.

Appleby grew angry and Wheeler grew angry. The talk was coming to a climax, both men were holding on to their tempers, but it was clear one or the other must give way soon.

Jeffrey Allen, about to go in search of Maida, saw a wisp of smoke curling from the garage, which from his seat on the north veranda was in plain view.

He ran toward the smoke, shouting "Fire!" as he ran, and in a few minutes the garage was ablaze. The servants gathered about, Mrs. Wheeler looked from her bedroom window, and Keefe joined Allen in attempts to subdue the flames.

And with the efficient help of two chauffeurs and other willing workers the fire was soon reduced to a smouldering heap of ashes.

Allen ran, then, to the den, to tell them there that the danger was past.

He entered to see Samuel Appleby dead in his chair, with a bullet through his heart. Daniel Wheeler stood beside him, gazing distractedly at the dead man. Maida, white and trembling, was half hidden as she stood just inside the curtains of the window.

Not realizing that there was no hope of life, Allen shouted for help, and tore open Appleby's coat to feel his heart.

"He's quite dead," he said, in an awe-stricken tone. "But, we must get a doctor at once!"

"I'll telephone," spoke up Genevieve's quiet voice, and with her usual efficiency, she found the number and called the doctor.

"Now the police?" she went on, as if such matters belonged to her province.

"Certainly," said Curtis Keefe, who stood by his late employer, taking charge, by common consent.

"Who killed him?" said Genevieve, in a hushed tone, as she left the telephone.

All looked from one to another, but nobody replied.

Mrs, Wheeler came to the doorway.

"I knew it!" she cried; "the phantom bugler!"

"But the phantom bugler didn't kill him," said Genevieve, "and we must find out who did!"

CHAPTER 7: INQUIRIES

Late the same evening the Wheeler family and their guests were gathered in the living-room. Much had been done in the past few hours. The family doctor had been there, the medical examiner had been called and had given his report, and the police had come and were still present.

Samuel Appleby, junior—though no longer to be called by that designation—was expected at any moment.

Two detectives were there, but one, Hallen by name, said almost nothing, seeming content to listen, while his colleague conducted the questioning of the household.

Burdon, the talkative one, was a quick-thinking, clear-headed chap, decided of manner and short of speech.

"Now, look here," he was saying, "this was an inside job, of course. Might have been one of the servants, or might have been any of you folks. How many of you are ready to help me in my investigations by telling all you know?"

"I thought we had to do that, whether we're ready to or not," spoke up Genevieve, who was not at all abashed by the presence of the authorities. "Of course, we'll all tell all we know—we want to find the murderer just as much as you do."

Keefe looked at her with a slight frown of reproof, but said nothing. The others paid no attention to the girl's rather forward speech.

In fact, everybody seemed dazed and dumb. The thing was so sudden and so awful—the possibilities so many and so terrible—that each was aghast at the situation.

The three Wheelers said nothing. Now and then they looked at one another, but quickly looked away, and preserved their unbroken silence.

Jeffrey Allen became the spokesman for them. It seemed inevitable—for some one must answer the first leading questions; and though Curtis Keefe and Miss Lane were in Appleby's employ, the detective seemed more concerned with the Wheeler family.

"Bad blood, wasn't there, between Mr. Appleby and Mr. Wheeler?" Burdon inquired.

"They had not been friends for years," Allen replied, straightforwardly, for he felt sure there was nothing to be gained by misrepresentation.

"Huh! What was the trouble, Mr. Wheeler?"

Daniel Wheeler gave a start. Then, pulling himself together, he answered slowly: "The trouble was that Mr. Appleby and myself belonged to different political parties, and when I opposed his election as governor, he resented it, and a mutual enmity followed which lasted ever since."

"Did you kill Mr. Appleby?"

Wheeler looked at his questioner steadily, and replied: "I have nothing to say."

"That's all right, you don't have to incriminate yourself."

"He didn't kill him!" cried Maida, unable to keep still. "I was there, in the room—I could see that he didn't kill him!"

"Who did then?" and the detective turned to her.

"I—I don't know. I didn't see who did it."

"Are you sure, Miss? Better tell the truth."

"I tell you I didn't see—I didn't see anything! I had heard an alarm of fire, and I was wondering where it was."

"You didn't get up and go to find out?"

"No—no, I stayed where I was."

"Where were you?"

"In the window-seat—in the den."

"Meaning the room where the shooting occurred?"

"Yes. My father's study."

"And from where you sat, you could see the whole affair?"

"I might have—if I had looked—but I didn't. I was reading."

"Thought you were wondering about the fire?"

"Yes," Maida was quite composed now. "I raised my eyes from my book when I heard the fire excitement."

"What sort of excitement?"

"I heard people shouting, and I heard men running. I was just about to go out toward the north veranda, where the sounds came from, when I—I can't go on!" and Maida broke down and wept.

"You must tell your story—maybe it'd be easier now than later. Can't you go on, Miss Wheeler?"

"There's little to tell. I saw Mr. Appleby fall over sideways—"

"Didn't you hear the shot?"

"No—yes—I don't know." Maida looked at her father, as if to gain help from his expression, but his face showed only agonized concern for her.

"Dear child," he said, "tell the truth. Tell just what you saw—or heard."

"I didn't hear anything—I mean the noise from the people running to the fire so distracted my attention, I heard no shot or any sound in the room. I just saw Mr. Appleby fall over—"

"You're not giving us a straight story, Miss Wheeler," said the detective, bluntly. "Seems to me you'd better begin all over."

"Seems to me you'd better cease questioning Miss Wheeler," said Curtis Keefe, looking sympathetically at Maida; "she's just about all in, and I think she's entitled to some consideration."

"H'm. Pretty hard to find the right one to question. Mrs. Wheeler, now—I'd rather not trouble her too much."

"Talk to me," said Allen. "I can tell you the facts, and you can draw your deductions afterward."

"Me, too," said Keefe. "Ask us the hard questions, and then when you need to, inquire of the Wheelers. Remember, they're under great nervous strain."

"Well, then," Burdon seemed willing to take the advice, "you start in, Mr. Keefe. You're Mr. Appleby's secretary, I believe?"

"Yes; we were on our way back to his home in Stockfield—we expected to go there to-morrow."

"You got any theory of the shooting?"

"I've nothing to found a theory on. I was out at the garage helping to put out a small fire that had started there."

"How'd it start?"

"I don't know. In the excitement that followed, I never thought to inquire."

"Tell your story of the excitement."

"I was at the garage with Mr. Allen, and two chauffeurs—the Wheelers' man and Mr. Appleby's man. Together, and with the help of a gardener or two, we put the fire out. Then Mr. Allen said: 'Let's go to the house and tell them there's no danger. They may be worried.' Mr. Allen started off and I followed. He preceded me into the den—"

"Then you tell what you saw there, Mr. Allen."

"I saw, first of all," began Jeffrey, "the figure of Mr. Appleby sitting in a chair, near the middle of the room. His head hung forward limply, and his whole attitude was unnatural. The thought flashed through my mind that he had had a stroke of some sort, and I went to him—and I saw he was dead."

"You knew that at once?"

"I judged so, from the look on his face and the helpless attitude. Then I felt for his heart and found it was still."

"You a doctor?"

"No; but I've had enough experience to know when a man is dead."

"All right. What was Mr. Wheeler doing?"

"Nothing. He stood on the other side of the room, gazing at his old friend."

"And Miss Wheeler?"

"She, too, was looking at the scene. She stood in the bay window."

"I see. Now, Mr. Keefe, I believe you followed close on Mr. Allen's heels. Did you see the place—much as he has described it?"

"Yes;" Keefe looked thoughtful. "Yes, I think I can corroborate every word of his description."

"All right. Now, Miss Lane, where were you?"

"I was at the fire. I followed the two men in, and I saw the same situation they have told you of."

Genevieve's quiet, composed air was a relief after the somewhat excited utterances of the others.

"What did you do?"

"I am accustomed to wait on Mr. Appleby, and it seemed quite within my province that I should telephone for help for him. I called the doctor—and then I called the police station."

"You don't think you took a great deal on yourself?"

Genevieve stared at him. "I do not think so. I only think that I did my duty as I saw it, and in similar circumstances I should do the same again."

At this point the other detective was heard from.

"I would like to ask," Hallen said, "what Mrs. Wheeler meant by crying out that it was the work of a 'phantom burglar'?"

"Not burglar—bugler," said Mrs. Wheeler, suddenly alert.

"Bugler!" Hallen stared. "Please explain, ma'am."

"There is a tradition in my family," Mrs. Wheeler said, in a slow, sad voice, "that when a member of the family is about to die, a phantom bugler makes an appearance and sounds 'taps' on his bugle. This phenomenon occurred last night."

"Oh, no! Spooks! But Mr. Appleby is not a member of your family."

"No; but he was under our roof. And so I know the warning was meant for him."

"Well, well, we can't waste time on such rubbish," interposed Burdon, "the bugle call had nothing to do with the case."

"How do you explain it, then?" asked Mrs. Wheeler. "We all heard it, and there's no bugler about here."

"Cut it out," ordered Burdon. "Take up the bugler business some other time, if you like—but we must get down to brass tacks now."

His proceedings were interrupted, however, by the arrival of young Samuel Appleby.

The big man came in and a sudden hush fell upon the group.

Daniel Wheeler rose—and put out a tentative hand, then half withdrew it as if he feared it would not be accepted.

Hallen watched this closely. He strongly suspected Wheeler was the murderer, but he had no intention of getting himself in bad by jumping at the conclusion.

However, Appleby grasped the hand of his host as if he had no reason for not doing so.

"I'm sorry, sir, you should have had this tragedy beneath your roof," he said.

Hallen listened curiously. It was strange he should adopt an apologetic tone, as if Wheeler had been imposed upon.

"Our sorrow is all for you, Sam," Dan Wheeler returned, and then as Appleby passed on to greet Maida and her mother, Wheeler sank back in his chair and was again lost in thought.

The whole scene was one of constraint. Appleby merely nodded to Genevieve, and spoke a few words to Keefe, and then asked to see his father.

On his return to the living-room, he had a slightly different air. He was a little more dictatorial, more ready to advise what to do.

"The circumstances are distressing," he said, "and I know, Mr. Wheeler, you will agree with me that we should take my father back to his home as soon as possible.

"That will be done to-morrow morning—as soon as the necessary formalities can be attended to. Now, anything I can do for you people, must be done to-night."

"You can do a lot," said Burdon. "You can help us pick out the murderer—for, I take it, you want justice done?"

"Yes—yes, of course." Appleby looked, surprised. "Of course I want this deed avenged. But I can't help in the matter. I understand you suspect some one of the—the household. Now, I shall never be willing to accuse any one of this deed. If it can be proved the work of an outsider—a burglar or highwayman—or intruder of any sort, I am ready to prosecute—but if suspicion rests on—on anyone I know—I shall keep out of it."

"You can't do that, Mr. Appleby," said Hallen; "you've got to tell all you know."

"But I don't know anything! I wasn't here!"

"You know about motives," Hallen said, doggedly. "Tell us now, who bore your father any ill-will, and also had opportunity to do the shooting?"

"I shan't pretend I don't know what you're driving at," and Appleby spoke sternly, "but I've no idea that Mr. Daniel Wheeler did this deed. I know he and my father were not on friendly terms, but you need more evidence than that to accuse a man of murder."

"We'll look after the evidence," Hallen assured him. "All you need tell about is the enmity between the two men."

"An enmity of fifteen years' standing," Appleby said, slowly, "is not apt to break out in sudden flame of crime. I am not a judge nor am I a detective, but until Mr. Wheeler himself confesses to the deed, I shall never believe he shot my father."

Wheeler looked at the speaker in a sort of dumb wonder.

Maida gazed at him with eyes full of thankfulness, and the others were deeply impressed by the just, even noble, attitude of the son of the victim of the tragedy.

But Hallen mused over this thing. He wondered why Appleby took such an unusual stand, and decided there was something back of it about which he knew nothing as yet. And he determined to find out.

"We can get in touch with you at any time, Mr. Appleby?" he asked.

"Oh, yes, of course. After a few days—after my father's funeral, I will be at your disposal. But as I've said, I know nothing that would be of any use as evidence. Do you need to keep Mr. Keefe and Miss Lane for any reason?"

"Why, I don't think so," the detective said. "Not longer than to-morrow, anyhow. I'll take their depositions, but they have little testimony to give. However, you're none of you very far away."

"No; you can always get us at Stockfield. Mr. Keefe will probably be willing to stay on and settle up my father's affairs, and I know we shall be glad of Miss Lane's services for a time." Appleby glanced at the two as he spoke, and they nodded,

"Well, we're going to stay right here," andBurdon spoke decidedly. "Whatever the truth of the matter may be, it's clear to be seen that suspicion must naturally point toward the Wheeler family, or some intruder. Though how an intruder could get in the room, unseen by either Mr. Wheeler or his. daughter, is pretty inexplicable. But those things we're here to find out. And we'll do it, Mr. Appleby. I'm taking it for granted you want the criminal found?"

"Oh—I say, Mr.—er—Burdon, have a little common decency! Don't come at me with questions of that sort, when I'm just about knocked out with this whole fearful occurrence! Have a heart, man, give me time to realize my loss, before you talk to me of avenging it!"

"That's right," said Curt Keefe. "I think Mr. Appleby deserves more consideration. Suppose we excuse him for the night."

Somewhat reluctantly the detective was brought to consent, and then Daniel Wheeler asked that he and his wife and daughter also be excused from further grilling that night.

"We're not going to run away," he said, pathetically. "We'll meet you in the morning, Mr. Burdon, but please realize our stunned condition at present."

"My mother must be excused," Maida put in, "I am sure she can stand no more," and with a solicitous care, she assisted Mrs. Wheeler to rise from her chair.

"Yes, I am ill," the elder woman said, and so white and weak did she look that no one could doubt her word.

The three Wheelers went to their room, and Genevieve Lane went off with them, leaving Allen and Keefe, with Sam Appleby, to face the two detectives' fire of questions.

"You vamoose, too, Sam," Keefe advised. "There's no use in your staying here and listening to harrowing details. Mr. Allen and I will have a talk with the detectives, and you can talk to-morrow morning, if you wish."

"All right," and Appleby rose. "But, look here, Keefe. I loved and respected my father, and I revere his memory— and, yes, I want justice done—of course, but, all the same, if Wheeler shot dad, I don't want that poor old chap prosecuted. You know, I never fully sympathized with father's treatment of him, and I'd like to make amends to Wheeler by giving him the benefit of the doubt—if it can be done."

"It can't be done!" declared Burdon, unwilling to agree to this heresy. "The law can't be set aside by personal sympathy, Mr. Appleby!"

"Well, I only said, if it can be," and the man wearily turned and left the room.

"Now, then," said Keefe, "let's talk this thing out. I know your position, Allen, and I'm sorry for you. And I want to say, right now, if I can help in any way, I will. I like the Wheelers, and I must say I subscribe to the ideas of Sam Appleby. But all that's up to the detectives. I've got to go away to-morrow, so I'm going to ask you, Mr. Burdon, to get through with me to-night. I've lots to do at the other end of the route, and I must get busy. But I do want to help here, too. So, at any rate, fire your questions at me—that is, if you know what you want to ask."

"I'll ask one, right off, Mr. Keefe," and Hallen spoke mildly but straightforwardly. "Can you give me any fact or suggest to me any theory that points toward any one but Mr. Daniel Wheeler as the murderer of Samuel Appleby?"

Curtis Keefe was dismayed. What could he reply to this very definite question? A negative answer implicated Wheeler at once—while a "yes," would necessitate the disclosure of another suspect. And Keefe was not blind to the fact that Hallen's eyes had strayed more than once toward Maida Wheeler with a curious glance.

Quickly making up his mind, Keefe returned: "No fact, but a theory based on my disbelief in Mr. Wheeler's guilt, and implying the intrusion of some murderous-minded person."

"Meaning some marauder?" Hallen looked disdainful.

"Some intruder," Keefe said. "I don't know who, or for what reason, but I don't think it fair to accuse Mr. Wheeler without investigating every possible alternative."

"There are several alternatives," Burdon declared; "I may as well say right out, that I've no more definite suspicion of Mr. Wheeler than I have of Mrs. Wheeler or Miss Wheeler."

"What!" and Jeffrey Allen looked almost murderous himself.

"Don't get excited, sir. It's my business to suspect. Suspicion is not accusation. You must admit all three of the Wheeler family had a motive. That is, they would, one and all, have been glad to be released from the thrall in which Mr. Appleby held them. And no one else present had a motive! I might suspect you, Mr. Allen, but that you were at the fire at the time, according to the direct testimony of Mr. Keefe."

"Oh, yes, we were at the fire, all right," Allen agreed, "and I'd knock you down for saying to me what you did, only you are justified. I would far rather be suspected of the murder of Mr. Appleby than to have any of the Wheelers suspected. But owing to Keefe's being an eye-witness of me at the time, I can't falsify about it. However, you may set it right down that none of the three Wheelers did do it, and I'll prove it!"

"Go to it, Allen," Keefe cried. "I'll help."

"You're two loyal friends of the Wheeler family," said Hallen in his quiet way, "but you can't put anything over. There's no way out. I know all about the governor's pardon and all that. I know the feud between the two men was beyond all hope of patching up. And I know that to-night had brought about a climax that had to result in tragedy. If Wheeler hadn't killed Appleby—Appleby would have killed Wheeler."

"Self-defence?" asked Allen.

"No, sir, not that. But one or the other had to be out of the running. I know the whole story, and I know what men will do in a political crisis that they wouldn't dream of at any other time. Wheeler's the guilty party—unless— well, unless that daughter of his—"

"Hush!" cried Allen. "I won't stand for it!"

"I only meant that the girl's great love and loyalty to her father might have made her lose her head—"

"No; she didn't do it," said Allen, more quietly. "Oh, I say, man, let's try to find this intruder that Mr. Keefe has—"

"Has invented!" put in Burdon. "No, gentlemen, they ain't no such animile! Now, you tell me over again, while

I take it down, just what you two saw when you came to the door of that den, as they call it."

And so Allen and Keefe reluctantly, but truthfully, again detailed the scene that met their eyes as they returned from the fire they had put out.

"The case is only too plain," declared Burdon, as he snapped a rubber band over his notebook. "Sorry, gentlemen, but your story leaves no loophole for any other suspect than one of the three Wheelers. Good-night."

Chapter 8: Confession

Before Sam Appleby left the next morning, he confided to Keefe that he had little if any faith in the detective prowess of the two men investigating the case.

"When I come back," he said, "I may bring a real detective, and—I may not. I want to think this thing over first-and, though I may be a queer Dick, I'm not sure I want the slayer of my father found."

"I see," and Keefe nodded his head understandingly.

But Jeffrey Allen demurred. "You say that, Mr. Appleby, because you think one of the Wheeler family is the guilty party. But I know better. I know them so well—"

"Not as well as I do," interrupted Appleby, "and neither do you know all the points of the feud that has festered for so many years. If you'll take my advice, Mr. Allen, you'll delay action until my return, at least."

"The detectives won't do that," objected Jeffrey.

"The detectives will run round in circles and get nowhere," scoffed Appleby. "I shall be back as soon as possible, and I don't mind telling you now that there will be no election campaign for me."

"What!" exclaimed Curtis Keefe. "You're out of the running?"

"Positively! I may take it up again some other year, but this campaign will not include my name."

"My gracious!" exclaimed Genevieve, who knew a great deal about current politics. "Who'll take your place?"

"A dark horse, likely," returned Appleby, speaking in an absorbed, preoccupied manner, as if caring little who fell heir to his candidacy.

"I don't agree with you, Mr. Appleby," spoke up Jeff Allen, "as to the inefficiency of the two men on this case. Seems to me they're doing all they can, and I can't help thinking they may get at the truth."

"All right, if they get at the truth, but it's my opinion that the truth of this matter is not going to be so easily discovered, and those two bunglers may do a great deal of harm. Good-bye, Maida, keep up a good heart, my girl."

The group on the veranda said good-bye to Sam Appleby, and he turned back he stepped into the car to say:

"I'll be back as soon as the funeral is over, and until then, be careful what you say—all of you."

He looked seriously at Maida, but his glance turned toward the den where Mr. Wheeler sat in solitude.

"I heard him," stormed Burdon, as the car drove away, and the detective came around the corner of the veranda. "I heard what he said about me and Hallen. Well, we'll show him! Of course, the reason he talks like that—"

"Don't tell us the reason just now," interrupted Keefe. "We men will have a little session of our own, without the ladies present. There's no call for their participation in our talk."

"That's right," said Allen. "Maida, you and Miss Lane run away, and we'll go to the den for a chat."

"No, not there," objected Burdon. "Come over and sit under the big sycamore."

And so, beneath the historic tree, the three men sat down for a serious talk. Hallen soon joined them, but he said little.

"I'm leaving myself, soon after noon," said Keefe. "I'll be back in a day or two, but there are matters of importance connected with Mr. Appleby's estate that must be looked after."

"I should think there must be!" exclaimed Burdon. "I don't see how you can leave to come back very soon."

Keefe reddened slightly, for the real reason for his intended return was centred in Maida Wheeler's charm, to which he had incontinently succumbed. He knew Allen was her suitor, but his nature was such that he believed in his own powers of persuasion to induce the girl to transfer her affections to his more desirable self.

But he only looked thoughtfully at Burdon and said: "There are matters here, also, that require attention in Mr. Appleby's interests."

"Well," Burdon went on, "as to the murder, there's no doubt that it was the work of one of the three Wheelers. Nobody else had any reason to wish old Appleby out of the world."

"You forget me," said Allen, in a tense voice. "My interests are one with the Wheelers. If they had such a motive as you ascribe to them—I had the same."

"Don't waste time in such talk," said Curt Keefe. "I saw you, Allen, at the fire during the whole time that covered the opportunity for the murder."

"Of course," agreed Burdon, "I've looked into" all that. And so, as I say, it must have been one member of the Wheeler family, for there's no one else to suspect."

"Including Mrs. Wheeler," quietly put in Hallen.

"How absurd!" flared out Allen. "It's bad enough to suspect the other two, but to think of Mrs. Wheeler is ridiculous!"

"Not at all," said Burdon, "she had the same motive—she had opportunity—"

"How do you know?" asked Keefe.

"She ran down from her room at that very moment," stated Burdon. "I have the testimony of one of the upstairs maids, and, also, I believe Miss Wheeler saw her mother in the den."

"Look here," said Hallen, in his slow, drawling tones, "let's reconstruct the situation. You two men were at the fire—that much is certain—so you can't be suspected. But all three of the Wheelers had absolute opportunity, and they had motive. Now, as I look at it—one of those three was the criminal, and the other two saw the deed.

Wherefore, the two onlookers will do all they can to shield the murderer."

Keefe stared at him. "You really believe that!" he said.

"Sure I do! Nobody else had either motive or opportunity. I don't for one minute believe in an outsider. Who could happen along at that particular moment, get away with the shooting, and then get away himself?"

"Why, it could have been done," mused Keefe, and Allen broke in eagerly:

"Of course it could! There's nothing to prove it impossible."

"You two say that, because you want it to be that way," said Burdon, smiling at the two young men. "That's all right—you're both friends of the family, and can't bear to suspect any one of them. But facts remain. Now, let's see which of the three it most likely was."

"The old man," declared Hallen, promptly.

"Nonsense!" cried Allen. "Mr. Wheeler is incapable of a deed like that! Why, I've known him for years—"

"Don't talk about incapable of anything!" said Burdon. "Most murderers are people whom their friends consider 'incapable of such a deed.' A man who is generally adjudged 'capable' of it is not found in polite society."

"Where's the weapon," asked Keefe, abruptly, "if Mr. Wheeler did it?"

"Where's the weapon, whoever did it?" countered Burdon. "The weapon hasn't been found, though I've hunted hard. But that helps to prove it one of the family, for they would know where to hide a revolver securely."

"If it was Mr. Wheeler, he'd have to hide it in the den," said Allen. "He never goes over to the other side of the house, you know."

"It isn't in the den," Hallen spoke positively; "I hunted that myself."

"You seem sure of your statement," said Keefe. "Couldn't you have overlooked it?"

"Positively not."

"No, he couldn't," concurred Burdon. "Hallen's a wonderful hunter. If that revolver had been hidden in the den, he'd have found it. That's why I think it was Mrs. Wheeler, and she took it back to her own rooms."

"Oh, not Mrs. Wheeler!" groaned Jeff Allen. "That dear, sweet woman couldn't—"

"Incapable of murder, I s'pose!" ironically said Burdon. "Let me tell you, sir, many a time a dear, sweet woman has done extraordinary things for the sake of her husband or children."

"But what motive would Mrs. Wheeler have?"

"The same as the others. Appleby was a thorn in their flesh, an enemy of many years' standing. And I've heard hints of another reason for the family's hating him, besides that conditional pardon business. But no matter about that now. What I want is evidence against somebody—against one of three suspects. Until I get some definite evidence I can't tell which of the three is most likely the one."

"Seems to me the fact that Mrs. Wheeler ran downstairs and back again is enough to indicate some pretty close questioning of her," suggested Hallen.

"Oh, please," begged Allen, "she's so upset and distracted—"

"Of course she is. But that's the reason we must ask her about it now. When she gets calmed down, and gets a fine yarn concocted, there'll be small use asking her anything!"

"I'd tackle the old man first," said Hallen; "I think, on general principles, he's the one to make inquiries of before you go to the ladies. Let's go to him now."

"No;" proposed Burdon, "let's send for him to come here. This is away from the house, and we can talk more freely."

"I'll go for him," offered Allen, seeing they were determined to carry out their plan.

"Not much!" said Burdon. "You're just aching to put a flea in his ear! You go for him, Hallen."

The detective went to the house, and returned with Daniel Wheeler at his side.

The suspected man stood straight and held himself fearlessly. Not an old man, he was grayed with care and trouble, but this morning he seemed strong and alert as any of them.

"Put your questions," he said, briefly, as he seated himself on one of the many seats beneath the old sycamore.

"First of all, who do you think killed Samuel Appleby?"

This question was shot at him by Burdon, and all waited in silence for the answer.

"I killed him myself," was the straightforward reply.

"That settles it," said Hallen, "it was one of the women."

"What do you mean by that?" cried Wheeler, turning quickly toward the speaker.

"I mean, that either your wife or daughter did the deed, and you are taking the crime on yourself to save her."

"No; "reasserted Dan Wheeler, "you're wrong. I killed Appleby for good and sufficient reason. I'm not sorry, and I accept my fate."

"Wait a minute," said Hallen, as Keefe was about to protest; "where was your daughter, Miss Maida, when you killed your man?"

"I—I don't know. I think she had gone to the fire—which had just broken out."

"You're not sure—"

"I am not."

"She had been with you, in the den?"

"I don't know."

"Well, I know. She had. She had been sitting in her favorite window-seat, in the large bay, and was there while you and Mr. Appleby were talking together. Also, she did not leave the room to go to the fire, for no one saw her anywhere near the burning garage."

"As to that, I can't say," went on Wheeler, slowly, "but she was not in the den, to my knowledge, at the time of the shooting."

"Very well, let that pass. Now, then, Mr. Wheeler, if you shot Mr. Appleby, what did you afterward do with your revolver?"

"I—I don't know." The man's face was convincing. His frank eyes testified to the truth of his words. "I assure you, I don't know. I was so—so bewildered—that I must have dropped it—somewhere. I never thought of it again."

"But if you had merely dropped it, it must have been found. And it hasn't been."

"Somebody else found it and secreted it," suggested Hallen. "Probably Mr. Wheeler's wife or daughter."

"Perhaps so," assented Wheeler, calmly. "They might have thought to help me by secreting it. Have you asked them?"

"Yes, and they deny all knowledge of it."

"So do I. But surely it will be found."

"It must be found. And, therefore, it is imperative that the rooms of the ladies as well as your own rooms, sir, be thoroughly searched."

"All right—go ahead and search!" Wheeler spoke sharply. "I've confessed the crime, now waste no time in useless chattering. Get the evidence, get the proofs, and let the law take its course."

"You will not leave the premises," put in Hallen, and his tone was that of command rather than inquiry.

"I most certainly shall not," declared Wheeler. "But I do ask you, gentlemen, to trouble and annoy my wife and daughter as little as possible. Their grief is sufficient reason for their being let alone."

"H'm," grunted Burdon. "Well, sir, I can promise not to trouble the ladies more than is necessary—but I can't help feeling necessity will demand a great deal."

Mrs. Wheeler was next interviewed, and the confab took place in her own sitting-room.

None of her family was allowed to be present, and the four men filed into the room with various expressions of face. The two detectives were stolid-looking, but eagerly determined to do their work, while Allen and Keefe were alertly interested in finding out some way to be of help to Mrs. Wheeler.

She received the men quietly, even graciously, sensing what they had come for.

"To start with, Mrs. Wheeler," said Burdon, frankly but not unkindly, "who do you think killed Mr. Appleby?"

"Oh—I don't know—I don't know," she wailed, losing her calm and becoming greatly agitated.

"Where were you when the shot was fired?" asked Hallen.

"I don't know—I didn't hear it—"

"Then you were up in your own room?"

"I suppose so—I don't know."

"You were up there when the fire broke out?"

"Yes—I think I was—"

"But you must know, Mrs. Wheeler—that is, you must know where you were when you first heard of the fire—"

"Yes, yes; I was up in my bedroom."

"And who told you of the fire?"

"My maid—Rachel."

"And then what did you do?"

"I—I—I don't remember."

"You ran downstairs, didn't you?"

"I don't remember—"

"Yes, you did!" Burdon took up the reins. "You ran downstairs,, and just as you got down to the den you saw—you saw your husband shoot Mr. Appleby!"

His harsh manner, as he intended, frightened the nervous woman, and reduced her to the verge of collapse.

But after a gasping moment, she recovered herself, and cried out: "I did not! I shot Mr. Appleby myself. That's why I'm so agitated."

"I knew it!" exclaimed Burdon. "Mr. Wheeler's confession was merely to save his wife. Now, Mrs.

Wheeler, I believe your story, and I want all the particulars. First, why did you kill him?"

"Be—because he was my husband's enemy—and I had stood it as long as I could."

"H'm. And what did you do with the weapon you used?"

"I threw it out of the window."

"And it dropped on the lawn?"

"Not dropped; I threw it far out—as far as I could."

"Oh, I see. Out of which window?"

"Why—why, the one in the den—the bay window."

"But your daughter—Miss Maida—was sitting in the bay window."

"No, she was not," Mrs. Wheeler spoke emphatically now. "She was not in the room at all. She had gone to the fire."

"Oh, is that so? And then—what happened next?"

"Why—nothing. I—I ran upstairs again."

"Appalled at what you had done?"

"Not appalled—so much as—as—"

"Unnerved?"

"Yes; unnerved. I fell on my bed, and Rachel looked after me."

"Ah, yes; we will interview Rachel, and so save you further harrowing details. Come on, men, let's strike while these irons are hot."

The four filed from the room, and Burdon spoke in a low tone, but excitedly:

"Come quickly! There goes Miss Maida across the lawn. We will take her next. The maid, Rachel, can wait."

Inwardly rebelling, but urged on by the others, Jeff Allen went along, and as Burdon stopped Maida, on her quick walk across the lawn, Jeff put his arm through that of the girl, and said: "Do as they tell you, dear. It's best to have this matter, settled at once."

Again the party grouped themselves under the old sycamore, and this time Maida was the target for their queries.

"Tell me all you know of the case," she said, peremptorily; "then I'll tell you what I know."

"We know that the murder was committed by one of you three Wheelers," said Burdon, brutally." Now, both your parents have confessed to being the criminal—"

"What?" Maida cried, her face white and her eyes big and frightened.

"Yes, ma'am, just that! Now, what have you to say? Are you going to confess also?"

"Of course I am! For I am the real criminal! Can't you see that my father and mother are both trying to shield me? I did it, because of that awful man's hold on my father! Take my confession, and do with me what you will!"

"Here's a state of things!" cried Burden, truly surprised at this new development.

"The girl is telling the truth," exclaimed Curtis Keefe, not because he really thought so but his quick mind told him that it would be easier to get a young girl acquitted than an older person, and he saw the plausibility of the detectives' theory that it must have been one of the three Wheelers.

"All right," Burden went on, "then, Miss Wheeler, enlighten us as to details. Where's the weapon?"

"I don't have to tell you anything except that I did it. Do I, Jeffrey? Do I, Mr. Keefe?" She looked at these two for help.

"No, Miss Wheeler," Keefe assured her, "you needn't say a word without legal advice."

"But, Maida," Jeffrey groaned, "you didn't do it—you know! You couldn't have!"

"Yes, I did, Jeff." Maida's eyes were glittering, and her voice was steady. "Of course I did. I'd do anything to save father from any more persecution by that man! And there was to be more!. Oh, don't let me talk! I mustn't!"

"No, you mustn't," agreed Keefe. "Now, Burdon, you've got three confessions! What are you going to do with them?"

"Going to find out which is the true one," answered Burdon, with a dogged expression. "I knew all the time it was one of the three, and I'm not surprised that the other two are willing to perjure themselves to save the criminal."

"Also, there may have been collusion," suggested Hallen.

"Of course," the other agreed. "But we'll find out. The whole thing rests among the three. They must not be allowed to escape—"

"I've no intention of running away!" said Maida, proudly.

"No one will run away," opined Hallen, sagaciously. "The criminal will stand by the other two, and the other two will stand by him."

"Or her, as the case may be," supplemented Burdon.

"Her," Maida assured him. "In the first place, my mother was upstairs in her own room, and my father was not in the den at the time. I was there alone."

"Oh, yes, your father was in the den," cried Jeffrey, imploringly.

"No," said Maida, not catching his meaning.

But Hallen caught it.

"Where was Mr. Wheeler?" he asked.

"I—I don't know," Maida said.

"Well, if he wasn't in the den, and if he wasn't upstairs, maybe he was in the big living-room, looking out at the fire."

"Yes—yes, I think he was!" Maida agreed.

"Then," Hallen went on, "then, Mr. Wheeler broke his parole—and is due for punishment."

"Oh, no," Maida moaned, seeing where her statements had led. "I—I guess he was in the den after all."

"And I guess you're making up as you go along," opined Mr. Hallen.

Chapter 9: Counter-Confessions

Before Keefe went away, young Allen had a serious talk with him.

"I want to ask your advice," Allen said; "shall I confess to that crime?"

"Man alive, what are you talking about?" Keefe cried, astounded at the suggestion.

"Talking sense," Jeffrey stoutly asserted. "I don't believe any one of those three did it—they're saying they did to shield one another—and so—"

"And so, you want to get into the game!" Keefe smiled at him. "You're very young, my boy, to think such crude methods would get over, even with such muffs as those two booby sleuths! No, Allen, don't add another perjury that can be of no possible use. You didn't do the killing, did you?"

"Of course not! But neither did the Wheelers!"

"No one of them?"

"Certainly not."

"Who did, then?"

"I don't know; but you yourself insisted on some marauder."

"Only to get suspicion away from the family. But there's no hope of finding any evidence of an outside job. You see, I've made some inquiries myself, and the servants' tales make it pretty sure that no intruder could have been here. So, the Wheelers are the only suspects left."

"And am I not as good for a suspect as they are—if I make doe confession?"

"No, Allen, you're not. You're in love with Miss Maida—"

"I'm engaged to her!"

"All right; don't you see, then, the absurdity of expecting any one to believe that you, a decent, law-abiding young citizen, would commit a murder which would positively render impossible a marriage with the girl you love?"

"I didn't think of that!"

"Of course you didn't. But that would make it unlikely that those detectives would believe your tale for a moment. No, it's ridiculous for any more people to confess to this murder. Three avowed criminals are quite enough for the crime!"

"But none of them really did it."

"How you harp on that string! Now, look here, Allen, I'm as loath to believe it as you are, but we must face facts. Those three people had motive and opportunity. Moreover, they're a most united family, and if any one thought either of the other two guilty, that one is quite capable of falsely avowing the crime."

"Yes—I see that"—Allen spoke impatiently. "What I want to know is, what we're going to do about it?"

"There I can't advise you. I have to get away now, but, as I said, I'll return. I've more than a little taste for investigation myself, and when I come back, I've no doubt I can hel—"

"But—Keefe—I don't want you to help—to investigate—if it's going to prove anything on any of the Wheelers."

"But you believe them innocent!"

"Yes; but crime has been fastened on the innocent."

"Look here, Allen, you do believe them innocent—but you fear your belief is a mistaken one!"

"God help me, I do fear that, Keefe! Oh, what can we do?"

"It's a bad lookout! All I can say now, is, to preserve a non-committal demeanor, and keep things stationary as much as you can. Maybe when I come back, we can—well, at least muddle things so—"

"Complicate the evidence! So that it won't indicate—"

"Be careful now! You know what compounding a felony means, don't you? Oh, Allen, you're so young and impulsive, and the Wheelers are so emotional and indiscreet, I wonder what will happen, before I get back!"

"Somebody ought to be in charge here."

"Yes, some good lawyer, or some level-headed person who would hold back those fool detectives, and look out for the interests of the Wheelers."

"I wish you could stay."

"I wish so, too, but I'll do all I can to return quickly. And Mr. Wheeler ought to be able to look after his own affairs!"

"I know he ought to—but he isn't. Also, I ought to, but I'm not!"

"Yes you are, Jeffrey," cried Maida, who had happened along in time to hear the young man's depreciation of himself.

"Hello, Maida," he turned to her. "What did you mean by making up that string of falsehoods?"

"Don't talk about it, Jeff," and the girl's face went white. "If you do, I shall go mad!"

"I don't wonder, Miss Wheeler," said Keefe, sympathetically. "Now, as I've just told Allen, I'm coming back as soon as I can make it, and until I do, won't you try to hold off those men? Don't let them pound you and your parents into admissions better left unmade. I'm not asking you any questions, I've no right to, but I beg of you to keep your own counsel. If you are shielding someone, say as little as possible. If you are guilty yourself, say nothing."

"' Guilty herself!' You've no right to say such a thing!" Allen cried out.

"Of course I have," Keefe returned, "when I heard Miss Wheeler avow the crime! But I must go now. Here's the car. Good-bye, both of you, and—Miss Wheeler, if I may advise, don't confide too much—in anybody."

The last words were spoken in an aside, and if Allen heard them he gave no sign. He bade Keefe good-bye with a preoccupied air, and as others joined them then, he waited till the car started, and then took Maida's arm and led her away, toward the garden.

Miss Lane, of course, went with Keefe, and as the girls parted Maida had suddenly felt a sense of loneliness.

"I liked Genevieve a lot," she said to Allen, as they walked away.

"I didn't," he returned.

"Oh, Jeff, you are so quick to take prejudices against people. I don't mean I'm specially fond of Genevieve, but she was kind to me, and now I do seem so alone."

"Alone, Maida? When you have your parents and me? What do you mean?"

"I can't tell you, exactly, but I seem to want someone—someone with wide experience and educated judgment—to whom I can go for advice."

"Won't I do, dear?"

"You're kind enough and loving enough—but, Jeff, you don't know things! I mean, you haven't had experience in—in criminal cases—"

"Come on, Maida, let's have it out. What about this criminal case of ours? For it's mine as much, as it's yours."

"Oh, no, it isn't, Jeff. You've nothing to do with it. I must bear my burden alone—and—I must ask you to release me from our engagement—"

"Which I will never do! How absurd! Now, Maida mine, if you won't speak out, I must. I know perfectly well you never killed Mr. Appleby. I know, too, that you saw either your father or mother kill him and you're trying to shield the criminal. Very right, too, except that you mustn't keep the truth from me. How can I help you, dear, unless I know what you're doing—or trying to do? So, tell me the truth—now."

"I can't tell you more than I have, Jeff," Maida spoke with a long-drawn sigh. "You must believe me. And as a— a murderer, I never, of course, shall marry."

"Maida, you're a transparent little prevaricator! Don't think I don't realize the awful situation, for I do, but I can't—I won't let you sacrifice yourself for either of your parents. I don't ask you which one it was—in fact, I'd rather you wouldn't tell me—but I do ask you to believe that I know it wasn't you. Now, drop that foolishness."

"Jeffrey," and Maida spoke very solemnly, "don't you believe that I could kill a man? If he was so cruel, so dangerous to my father—my dear father, that I couldn't stand it another minute, don't you believe I'd be capable of killing him?"

"We've spoken of that before, Maida, and I think I said I believed you would be capable, in a moment of sudden, intense anger and excitement—"

"Well, then, why do you doubt my word? I told the detectives—I tell you, that the moment came—I saw my father, under stress of terrible anger—in immediate, desperate danger from Samuel Appleby. I—I shot—to kill—" the girl broke down and Jeffrey took the slender, quivering form in his arms.

"All right, sweetheart," he whispered, "don't say another word—I understand. I don't blame you—how could you think I would! I just want to help you. How can I best do that?"

But Maida could not tell him. Her tears, once started, came in torrents. Her whole frame shook with the intensity of her sobs, and, unable to control herself at all, she ran from him into the house and up to her own room.

"What did you find out?" Burdon asked, coming out from behind a nearby clump of shrubbery.

"You sneak, you cad!" Allen cried, but the detective stopped him.

"Now, look here, Mr. Allen," he said, "we're here to do our duty, said duty being to discover the perpetrator of a pretty awful crime. You may be so minded as to let the murderer go scot-free, even help him or her to make a getaway, but I can't indulge in any such philanthropic scheme. Mr. Appleby's been foully murdered, and it's up to the law to find out the killer and see justice done. My job is not a pleasant one, but I've got to see it through, and that's all there is about that! Now, this case is what we call open-and-shut. The murderer is sure and positively one of three people—said three people being known to us. So, I've just got to use all my powers to discover which of the three I'm really after, and when I find that out, then make my arrest. But I've no desire to nab the wrong one"

"Which one do you think it is?" demanded Allen, angrily.

"I've got no right nor reason to think it's either one. I've got to find out for sure, not just think it. So, I ask you what you learned just now from Miss Wheeler, and why did she run to the house, weeping like a willow tree?"

"I found out nothing that would throw any light on your quest, and she wept because her nerves are strained to the breaking point with worry and exhaustion."

"And I don't wonder!" the detective spoke sympathetically. "But all the same, I'm obliged to keep on investigating, and I must ask you what she said to you just now."

Allen thought over the conversation he had had with Maida. Then he said: "I am telling the truth when I say there was no word said between us that would be of any real use to you. Miss Wheeler is my fiancee, and I tried to comfort her, and also to assure her anew of my faithfulness and devotion in her trouble."

"And what did she say?"

"Without remembering her words exactly, I think I can state that she said nothing more than to reiterate that she had killed Mr. Appleby. But I want to state also, that I believe she said it, as she said it to you, to shield some one else."

"Her parents—or, one of them?"

"That is the reasonable supposition. But I do not accuse either of the elder Wheelers. I still suspect an intruder from outside."

"Of course you do... Anybody in your position would. But there was none such. It was one of the three Wheelers, and I'll proceed to find out which one."

"Just how do you propose to find out?"

"Well, the one that did it is very likely to give it away. It's mighty difficult to be on your guard every minute, and with one guilty, and two shielding, and all three knowing, which is which, as I've no doubt they do, why, it's a cinch that one of the three breaks down through sheer over carefulness pretty soon."

"That's true enough," Allen agreed, ruefully. "Is that your only plan?"

"Yes, except to look up the weapon. It's a great help, always, to find the revolver."

"Hoping to find the criminal's initials on it?"

"Well, no, they don't mark firearms in real life, as they do in story-books. But to find the weapon gives a lot of evidence as to where it was fired from, and what was done with it afterward, and to whom it belongs. Not that the owner is always the murderer. More often the reverse is true. But the weapon we want and want pretty badly. By the way, I'm told that young Appleby is out of the running for governor now that his father isn't here to help him through."

"More, I take it, because of his grief for his father's untimely end."

"Be that as it may, he'll withdraw his name from the candidates."

"Who told you?"

"I heard Mr. Keefe telling Miss Lane."

"You hear a lot, Burdon."

"I do, Mr. Allen. It's my business to do so. Now, here's another thing. About that garage fire."

"Well, what about it?"

"It was a mighty mysterious fire, that's all. Nobody knows how it started, or where."

"They must know where!"

"Not exactly. It seemed to start in the vicinity of Mr. Appleby's own car. But there was nothing inflammable around that part of the garage."

"Well, what does that prove or indicate? Anything prejudicial to the Wheelers?"

"Not so far as I can see. Only it's queer, that's all."

"Perhaps Mr. Appleby kept tobacco and matches in his car."

"Perhaps so. Anyway, that's where the fire originated, and also about where it stopped. They soon put it out."

"Glad they did. I can't see that the fire has any bearing whatever on the murder."

"Neither can I, Mr. Allen. But Hallen, now, he thinks it has."

"Just how?"

"I can't say. Hallen doesn't know himself. But he says there's a connection."

"There may be. But unless it's a connection that will free the Wheelers from suspicion, it doesn't interest me."

Allen left the detective, who made no effort to detain him, and went to the den for a talk with Mr. Wheeler.

But that gentleman, locked in the room, declared through the closed door that he would see nobody.

"Sorry, Jeff," he said, in a kindly tone, "but you must excuse me at present. Give me the day to myself. I'll see you late this afternoon."

As it was already noon, Allen made no further attempt at an interview and went in search of Mrs. Wheeler. It seemed to him he must talk to some of the family, and he hadn't the heart to disturb Maida, who might be resting.

Mrs. Wheeler's maid said that her mistress would see him in a few minutes. And it was only a few minutes later that the lady came downstairs and greeted Allen, who awaited her in the living-room.

"What are we going to do?" she exclaimed to him. "Do help us, Jeff. Did I do right?"

"In lying to save some one you love? Yes, I suppose so."

But Sara Wheeler had very acute hearing. Even as they spoke, she heard a slight movement on the porch outside, and realized at once that a detective was listening to her every word.

Allen couldn't be sure whether this changed her mental attitude or whether she continued as she had meant to when she began.

But she said: "Oh, I don't mean that! I mean, did I do right to confess my crime at once? You know they would discover it sooner or later, and I thought it would save time and trouble for me to own up immediately."

"Dear Mrs. Wheeler, don't quibble with me. I know you didn't do it—"

"Oh, yes, I did, Jeff. Who else could it have been? And, too, you know about the bugler, don't you?"

"Yes."

"Well, that's what made me do it. You see, I thought if a death occurred, that would be the death the bugler was heralding, and if it wasn't Mr. Appleby it might have been Dan himself."

She leaned forward as she spoke, her voice dropped to a mere whisper, and her large eyes took on a glassy stare, while her white face was drawn and set with an agonized expression as of a dreadful memory.

"And you killed Appleby for that reason?" cried Allen.

"Oh, no—I killed him because—because "—her mind seemed to wander—" oh, yes," she resumed, "because he was a menace to Dan. To my husband."

For the first time Allen began to doubt her sanity. Her eyes were wild, her fingers nervously interlaced and her speech was jerky and stammering.

"A menace, how?" he asked, softly.

"In different ways," Mrs. Wheeler returned, in so low a voice that the listener outside could scarcely hear. "Through me, because of something he knew; through Maida—because of—of something he wanted; and, of course, through Dan himself, because of that old conditional pardon."

"What do you mean about Maida?" Allen caught at the thing that most impressed him. "Did old Appleby want to marry Maida?"

"Yes, he did. Of course, neither her father nor I would hear of such a thing, but Mr. Appleby was an insistent man—insistent and inexorable—and he wanted Maida—"

"Mother dear, I want you to come away now," and Maida came into the room. "Come, you have talked too long. It does no good, to you or to any one else. Did you call her down, Jeffrey?"

"Yes," and Allen deeply regretted his act. "But I want to talk to somebody, Maida. Will you take your mother away—and return?"

"Yes, I will," and the girl left the room, guiding the slow footsteps of her mother.

When she came back, Allen took her out under the old sycamore.

"Now, Maida," he said, gently, "the truth. No matter what it is, you must tell me. We are here alone, that eavesdropping detective can't overhear us, and you must tell me whom you are shielding and the full details for the crime."

"I can't tell you all the details, Jeff," the girl returned, "they include a secret that is not mine to divulge."

"You can divulge anything in a crisis like this, Maida."

"No, I cannot. Before he—before he died, Mr. Appleby told me something that I will never tell, unless my conscience makes me do so."

"Isn't it a matter of conscience already?"

"I don't know, Jeff; truly, I can't tell. But much as I am bound by my principles of right, and you know, dear, I am conscientious, I would willingly throw them all to the winds if they interfered with my parents' happiness, well-being or safety."

"Let me get this straight, Maida. You would stifle your conscience, would act directly against its dictates for the sake of your parents?"

"Yes, Jeffrey; right or wrong, that's what I should do."

"Who am I that I should judge you, dear? I know well your lifelong submission to your conscience, even when your inclinations were strong the other way. Now, if you have thrown over principle, honor, conscience and right, for what you consider a stronger motive, I can only accept your decision. But I wish you would confide in me more fully. Do you mean in regard to Mr. Appleby?"

"Of course I mean in regard to Mr. Appleby. And I'm going to ask you, Jeff, to believe what I tell you."

"Of course I'll do that, Maida."

"No; you won't want to. But I ask you to believe it implicitly and to act accordingly. Do you promise me this?"

The girl's face was turned to his, her great, sorrowful eyes were full of dumb agony and showed unshed tears, but her voice was clear and strong as of one whose purpose was unshakable.

"Yes, dear," and Jeffrey took her hands in his and looked deep into her eyes, whose blank despair haunted him long after, "yes, Maida, I promise."

"Well, then, I killed Mr. Appleby, and you must do whatever you think best for us all. What shall we do first, Jeffrey?"

And with the clutch of an icy dread at his heart, Allen replied, brokenly, "I don't know, Maida, darling, but I will find out what is best, and we will do it—"

Chapter 10: The Phantom Bugler

The day after the funeral of Samuel Appleby, Keefe returned to Sycamore Ridge.

"I came, Mr. Wheeler," he said, "to offer you my services. I express no opinion as to who killed Mr. Appleby, but I do know that his son is going to use every means to discover his father's murderer, and I can't help thinking you'd be wise to let me take up your case."

"As a criminal lawyer?" asked Dan Wheeler, quietly.

"No, sir; as a friend and adviser. If you find you need a criminal lawyer, I'll suggest one—and a good one. But I mean, I'd like to help you in a general way, by consultation and advice. You, if you will pardon me, have lived so long out of the modern world that you are unfitted to cope with this whole situation. I speak frankly—because I am deeply interested—"

"Just why are you so deeply interested, Mr. Keefe?" Wheeler's tone was kindly but his glance was sharp at his would-be benefactor.

"I may as well own up," Keefe said, "I am hard hit by your daughter. Oh, yes, I know she is engaged to young Allen, and I've no hope she would ever throw him over for me, but I'm anxious to serve her in any way I can—and I feel pretty sure that I can be of help to you and your family."

"Well spoken, young man. And your promises are right. I am out of touch with the world, and I should be glad indeed of the advice of an experienced man of business. But, first of all, will you tell me who you think killed Appleby?"

"I will, sir. I've no idea it was any of you three people, who have all confessed to the deed, in order to shield one another."

"Whom then do you suspect?"

"An outside intruder. I have held to this theory from the start, and I am sure it is the true one. Moreover, I think the murderer is the man who blew the bugle—"

"The phantom bugler!"

"No phantom, but a live man. Phantoms do not blow on bugles except in old English legends. A bugle sounded in New England and heard by several people, was blown by human lungs. Find your bugler and you've found your murderer."

"I wonder if you can be right!"

Wheeler fell into a brown study and Keefe watched him closely. His bugler theory was offered in an effort to find out what Wheeler thought of it, and Wheeler's response ought to show whether his own knowledge of the murder precluded the bugler or not.

Apparently it did, for he sighed and said: "Of course the person who sounded that bugle was a live person, but I cannot think it had any connection with Mr. Appleby's death. Even granting somebody might have been wicked enough to try to frighten my wife, yet there is no reason to think any one wishing to kill Samuel Appleby would know of the old legend in Mrs. Wheeler's family."

"True enough. But it is possible, and, in my opinion, that is the only direction to look."

"But what direction? How can you find out who blew that bugle?"

"I don't know yet, but I shall try to find out. As a matter of fact very little inquiry has been made. Those two detectives, while intelligent enough, don't have a very wide horizon. They've concluded that the assassin was— well, was named Wheeler—and they're only concerned to discover the first name. Forgive my plain speaking, but to save yourself and the other two, we must be outspoken."

"Yes, yes—pray don't hesitate to say anything you think. I am in a terrible position, Mr. Keefe—more terrible than you can know, and while I am willing to make any sacrifice for my dear ones—it may be in vain—"

The two men had been alone in the den, but now were joined by Burdon and young Allen.

"Glad to see you back, Mr. Keefe," Burdon said; "usually we detectives don't hanker after outside help, but you've a good, keen mind, and I notice you generally put your finger on the right spot."

"All right, Burdon, we'll work together. Now, Mr. Wheeler, I'm going to ask you to leave us—for there are some details to discuss—"

Dan Wheeler was only too glad to be excused, and with a sigh of relief he went away to his upstairs quarters.

"Now, it's this way," Keefe began; "I've been sounding Mr. Wheeler, but I didn't get any real satisfaction. But here's a point. Either he did or didn't kill Mr. Appleby, but in either case, he's in bad."

"What do you mean?" asked Allen.

"Why, I've inquired about among the servants and, adding our own testimony, I've figured it out that Mr. Wheeler was either the murderer or he was over the line on the other side of the house, and in that case has broken his parole and is subject to the law."

"How do you prove that?" inquired Burdon, interestedly.

"By the story of Miss Wheeler, who says her father was not in the den at all at the time Mr. Appleby was shot. Now, as we know, Mrs. Wheeler ran downstairs at that time, and she, too, says her husband was not in the den. Also she says he was not in the living-room, nor in the hall. This leaves only her own sitting-room, from which Mr. Wheeler could see the fire and into which he was most likely to go for that purpose."

"He wouldn't go in that room for any purpose," declared Allen.

"Not ordinarily, but in the excitement of a fire, men can scarcely refrain from running to look at it, and if he was not in the places he had a right to be, he must have been over on the forbidden ground. So, it comes back to this: either Mr. Wheeler was the murderer, and his wife and daughter have perjured themselves to save him, or he was in a place which, by virtue of the conditions, cancels his pardon. This, I take it, explains Mr. Wheeler's present perturbed state of mind—for he is bewildered and worried in many ways."

"Well," said Allen, "where does all this lead us?"

"It leads us," Keefe returned, "to the necessity of a lot of hard work. I'm willing to go on record as desiring to find a criminal outside of the Wheeler family. Or to put it bluntly, I want to acquit all three of them—even if—"

"Even if one of them is guilty?" said Burdon. "Well, yes—just that. But, of course I don't mean to hang an innocent man! What I want is to get a verdict for persons unknown."

"I'm with you," said Allen. "It's all wrong, I know, but—well, I can't believe any of the Wheelers really did it."

"You do believe it, though!" Keefe turned on him, sharply. "And what's more, you believe the criminal is the one of the three whom you least want it to be!"

Keefe's meaning was unmistakable, and Allen's flushed and crestfallen face betrayed his unwilling assent. Unable to retort—even unable to speak, he quickly left the room.

Keefe closed the door and turned to Burdon.

"That was a test," he said; "I'm not sure whether Allen suspects Miss Wheeler—or not—"

"He sure acts as if he does," Burdon said, his face drawn with perplexity. "But, I say, Mr. Keefe, haven't you ever thought it might have been Jeffrey Allen himself?"

"Who did the shooting?"

"Yes; he had all the motives the others had—"

"But not opportunity. Why, he was at the garage fire—where I was—"

"Yes, but he might have got away long enough for—"

"Nonsense, man, nothing of the sort! We were together, fighting the flames. The two chauffeurs were with us—the Wheelers' man, and Mr. Appleby's. We used those chemical extinguishers—"

"I know all that—but then—he might have slipped away, and in the excitement you didn't notice—"

"Not a chance! No, take my word for it, the three Wheelers are the exclusive suspects—unless we can work in that bugler individual."

"It's too many for me," Burdon sighed. "And Hallen, he's at his wit's end. But you're clever at suck things, sir, and Mr. Appleby, he's going to get a big detective from the city."

"You don't seem to mind being discarded!"

"No, sir. If anybody's to fasten a crime on one of those Wheelers, I don't want to be the one to do it."

"Look here, Burdon, how about Wheeler's doing it in self-defence? I know a lot about those two men, and Appleby was just as much interested in getting Wheeler out of his way as vice versa. If Appleby attacked and Wheeler defended, we can get him off easy."

"Maybe so, but it's all speculation, Mr. Keefe. What we ought to get is evidence—testimony—and that's hard, for the only people to ask about it are—"

"Are the criminals themselves."

"The suspected criminals-yes, sir."

"There are others. Have you quizzed all the servants?"

"I don't take much stock in servants' stories."

"You're wrong there, my man. That principle is a good one in ordinary matters, but when it comes to a murder case, a servant's testimony is as good as his master's."

Burdon made no direct response to Keefe's suggestion, but he mulled it over in his slow-going mind, and as a result, he had a talk with Rachel, who was ladies' maid to both Maida and her mother.

The girl bridled a little when Burdon began to question her.

"Nobody seemed to think it worth while to ask me anything," she said, "so I held my tongue. But if so be you want information, you ask and I'll answer."

"I doubt if she really knows anything," Burdon thought to himself, judging from her air of self-importance, but he said:

"Tell me anything you know of the circumstances at the time of the murder."

"Circumstances?" repeated Rachel, wrinkling her brow.

"Yes; for instance, where was Mrs. Wheeler when you heard the shot?"

"I didn't say I heard the shot."

"Didn't you?"

"Yes,"

"Go on, then; don't be foolish, or you'll be sorry for it!"

"Well, then, Mrs. Wheeler was downstairs-she had just left her room—"

"Here, let me get this story straight. How long had she been in her room? Were you there with her?"

"Yes; we had been there half an hour or so. Then, we heard noise and excitement and a cry of fire. Mrs. Wheeler rushed out of her room and ran downstairs—and I followed, naturally."

"Yes; and what did you see?"

"Nothing special—I saw a blaze of light, through the front door—"

"The north door?"

"Of course—the one toward the garage—and I saw the garage was on fire, so I thought of nothing else—then."

"Then? What did you think of later?"

"I remembered that I saw Mr. Wheeler in the living-room—in the north end of it—where he never goes—"

"You know about his restrictions?"

"Oh, yes, sir. The servants all know—we have to. Well, it was natural, poor man, that he should go to look at the fire!"

"You're sure of this, Rachel?"

"Sure, yes; but don't let's tell, for it might get the master in trouble."

"On the contrary it may get him out of trouble. To break his parole is not as serious a crime as murder. And if he was in the north end of the living-room he couldn't have been in the den shooting Mr. Appleby."

"That's true enough. And neither could Mrs. Wheeler have done it."

"Why not?"

"Well—that is—she was right ahead of me—"

"Did you keep her in sight?"

"No; I was so excited myself, I ran past her and out to the garage."

"Who was there?"

"Mr. Allen and Mr. Keefe and the two chauffeurs and the head gardener and well, most all the servants. The men were fighting the fire, and the women were standing back, looking on."

"Yelling, I suppose."

"No; they were mostly quiet. Cook was screaming, but nobody paid any attention to her."

"The fire was soon over?"

"Yes, it was a little one. I suppose that chauffeur of Mr. Appleby's dropped a match or something—for our servants are too well trained to do anything of the sort. We're all afraid of fire."

"Well, the fire amounted to little, as you say. Curious it should occur at the time of the murder."

"Curious, indeed, sir. Do you make anything out of that?"

"Can't see anything in it. Unless the murderer started the fire to distract attention from himself. In that case, it couldn't have been any of the Wheelers."

"That it couldn't. They were all in the house."

"Miss Maida—did you see her at the time?"

"I caught a glimpse of her as I ran through the hall."

"Where was she?"

"In the den; standing near the bay window." "Well, we've pretty well planted the three. Mrs. Wheeler on the

stairs, Mr. Wheeler, you say, in the living-room, where he
had no right to be, and Miss Maida—"

"Oh, Miss Maida didn't do it! She couldn't! That lovely
young lady!"

"There, Rachel, that will do. You've given, your
testimony, now it's not for you to pass judgment. Go
about your business, and keep a quiet tongue. No
babbling—you understand?"

"Yes, sir," and the maid went away, her attitude still
one of importance and her face wearing a vague smile.

Meantime Curtis Keefe was having a serious talk
with Maida.

His attitude was kindly and deferential, but he spoke
with a determined air as he said:

"Miss Wheeler, you know, I am sure, how much I
want to help you, and how glad I will be if I can do so.
But, first of all I must ask you a question. What did Mr.
Appleby mean when he said to you something about
Keefe and the airship?"

Maida looked at him with a troubled glance. For a
minute she did not speak, then she said, calmly: "I am not
at liberty to tell you what we were talking about then,
Mr. Keefe, but don't you remember Mr. Appleby said that
you were not the Keefe referred to?"

"I know he said that, but-I don't believe it."

"I am not responsible for your disbelief," she drew
herself up with a dignified air. "And I must ask you not to
refer to that matter again."

"Don't take that attitude," he begged. "At least tell me
what Keefe he did mean. There can be no breach of
confidence in that."

"Why do you want to know?"

"Because I know Mr. Appleby had a big airship project
under consideration. Because I know he contemplated
letting me in on the deal, and it was a most profitable
deal. Had he lived, I should have asked him about it, but
since he is dead, I admit I want to know anything you can
tell me of the matter."

Involuntarily Maida smiled a little, and the lovely face, usually so sad, seemed more beautiful than ever to the man who looked at her.

"Why do you smile?" he cried, "but whatever the reason, keep on doing so! Oh, Maida, how wonderful you are!"

A glance of astonishment made him quickly apologize for his speech.

"But," he said, "I couldn't help it. Forgive me, Miss Wheeler, and, since you can smile over it, I'm more than ever anxious to know about the airship deal."

"And I can tell you nothing," she declared, "because I know nothing of any such matter. If Mr. Appleby was interested in an airship project, I know nothing of it. The matter he mentioned to me was, I am positively certain, not the deal you speak of."

"I believe that. Your face is too honest for you to speak an untruth so convincingly. And now assure me that I am not the Keefe he referred to, and I will never open the subject again."

But this Maida could not say truthfully, and though she tried, her assertion was belied by drooping eyes and quivering lips.

"You were not," she uttered, but she did not look at him, and this time Curtis Keefe did not believe her.

"I was," he said calmly, but he made no further effort to get the whole truth from her. "I'm sorry you can't confide fully in me, but I shall doubtless learn all I want to know from Mr. Appleby's papers."

"You—you have them in charge?" Maida asked, quite evidently agitated at the thought.

"Yes, of course, I'm his confidential secretary. That's why, Miss Wheeler, it's better for you to be frank with me—in all things. Has it never occurred to you that I'm the man who can best help you in this whole moil of troubles?"

"Why, no," she said, slowly, "I don't believe it ever has."

"Then realize it now. Truly, dear Miss Wheeler, I am not only the one who can best help you, but I am the only one who can help you at all—please try to see that."

"Why should I want help?"

"For half a dozen very good reasons. First, I suppose you know that you are in no enviable position regarding the death of Mr. Appleby. Oh, I know you didn't kill him—"

"But I did!"

"If you did, you couldn't take it so calmly—"

"How dare you say I take it calmly? What do you know about it? Just because I don't go about in hysterics—that's not my nature—is no sign that I'm not suffering tortures—"

"You poor, sweet child—I know you are! Oh, little girl, dear little girl—can't you—won't you let me look out for you—"

The words were right enough, but the tone in which they were uttered, the look that accompanied them, frightened Maida. She knew at once how this man regarded her.

Intuition told her it was better not to resent his speech or meaning, so she only said, quietly:

"Look out for me—how?"

"Every way. Give yourself to me—be my own, own little Maida—"

"Mr. Keefe, stop! You forget you are talking to an engaged girl—"

"I did forget—please forgive me." In a moment he was humble and penitent. "I lost my head. No, Miss Wheeler, I ask no reward, I want to help you in any and every way—remembering you are to be the bride of Mr. Allen."

"Only after I'm acquitted of this crime. They never convict a woman, do they, Mr. Keefe?"

"So that's what you're banking on! And safely, too. No, Miss Wheeler, no judge or jury would ever convict you of murder. But, all the same, it's a mighty unpleasant process that brings about your acquittal, and I advise you not to go through with it."

"But I've got to. I've confessed my crime; now they have to try me—don't they?"

"You innocent baby. Unless—look here, you're not—er—stringing me, are you?"

"What does that mean?"

"I mean, you didn't really do the job, did you?"

"I did." The calm glance of despair might have carried conviction to a less skeptical hearer, but Keefe only looked puzzled.

"I can't quite make you out," he declared; "either you're a very brave heroine—or—"

"Or?" queried Maida.

"Or you're nutty!"

Maida laughed outright. "That's it," she said, and her laughter became a little hysterical. "I am nutty, and I own up to it. Do you think we can enter a plea of insanity?"

Keefe looked at her, a new thought dawning in his mind.

"That might not be at all a bad plan," he said, slowly; "are you in earnest?"

"I don't know. Honestly, I think of so many plans, and discard them one after the other. But I don't want to be convicted!"

"And you shan't! There are more persons in this world than the three Wheelers! And one of them may easily be the murderer we're seeking."

"Which one?" asked Maida.

"The Phantom Bugler," returned Keefe.

CHAPTER 11: FLEMING STONE

Next day brought the advent of two men and a boy to Sycamore Ridge.

Samuel Appleby, determined to discover the murderer of his father and convinced that it was none of the Wheeler family, had brought Fleming Stone, the detective, to investigate the case. Stone had a young assistant who always accompanied him, and this lad, Terence McGuire by name, was a lively, irrepressible chap, with red hair and freckles.

But his quick thinking and native wit rendered him invaluable to Stone, who had already hinted that McGuire might some day become his successor.

The Wheeler family, Jeffrey Allen, Curtis Keefe, and Burdon, the local detective, were all gathered in Mr. Wheeler's den to recount the whole story to Fleming Stone.

With grave attention, Stone listened, and young McGuire eagerly drank in each word, as if committing a lesson to memory. Which, indeed, he was, for Stone depended on his helper to remember all facts, theories and suggestions put forward by the speakers.

Long experience had made Fleming Stone a connoisseur in "cases," and, by a classification of his own, he divided them into "express" and "local." By this distinction he meant that in the former cases, he arrived quickly at the solution, without stop or hindrance. The latter kind involved necessary stops, even side issues, and a generally impeded course, by reason of conflicting motives and tangled clues.

As he listened to the story unfolded by the members of the party, he sighed, for he knew this was no lightning express affair. He foresaw much investigation ahead of him, and he already suspected false evidence and perhaps bribed witnesses.

Yet these conclusions of his were based quite as much on intuition as on evidence, and Stone did not wholly trust intuition.

Samuel Appleby was the principal spokesman, as he was the one chiefly concerned in the discovery of the criminal and the avenging of his father's death. Moreover, he was positive the deed had not been done by any one of the Wheeler family, and he greatly desired to prove himself right in this.

"But you were not here at the time, Mr. Appleby," Stone said, "and I must get the story from those who were. Mr. Keefe, you came with Mr. Appleby, senior, and, also, as his confidential secretary you are in a position to know of his mental attitudes. Had he, to your knowledge, any fear, any premonition of evil befalling him?"

"Not at all," answered Keefe, promptly. "If he had, I do not know of it, but I think I can affirm that he had not. For, when Mr. Appleby was anxious, he always showed it. In many ways it was noticeable, if he had a perplexity on his mind. In such a case he was irritable, quick-tempered, and often absent-minded. The day we came down here, Mr. Appleby was genial, affable and in a kindly mood. This, to my mind, quite precludes the idea that he looked for anything untoward."

"How did he impress you, Mr. Wheeler?" Stone went on. "You had not seen him for some time, I believe."

"Not for fifteen years," Dan Wheeler spoke calmly, and with an air of determined reserve. "Our meeting was such as might be expected between two long-time enemies, but Appleby was polite and so was I."

"He came to ask a favor of you?"

"Rather to drive a bargain. He offered me a full pardon in return for my assistance in his son's political campaign. You, I am sure, know all this from Mr. Appleby, the son."

"Yes, I do; I'm asking you if Mr. Appleby, the father, showed in his conversation with you, any apprehension or gave any intimation of a fear of disaster?"

"Mr. Stone," returned Wheeler, "I have confessed that I killed Mr. Appleby; I hold, therefore, that I need say nothing that will influence my own case."

"Well, you see, Mr. Wheeler, this case is unusual—perhaps unique, in that three people have confessed to the crime. So far, I am preserving an open mind. Though it is possible you and your wife and daughter acted in collusion, only one of you could have fired the fatal shot; yet you all three claim to have done so. There is no conclusion to be drawn from this but that one is guilty and the other two are shielding that one."

"Draw any conclusion you wish," said Wheeler, still imperturbably. "But I've no objection to replying to the question you asked me. Sam Appleby said no word to me that hinted at a fear for his personal safety. If he had any such fear, he kept it to himself."

"He knew of your enmity toward him?"

"Of course. He did me an unforgivable injustice and I never pretended that I did not resent it."

"And you refused to meet his wishes regarding his son's campaign?"

"I most certainly did, for the same reasons I opposed his own election many years ago."

"Yes; all those details I have from Mr. Appleby, junior. Now, Mr. Appleby does not believe that his father was killed by any member of your family, Mr. Wheeler."

"Can he, then, produce the man whom he does suspect?"

"No; he suspects no one definitely, but he thinks that by investigation, I can find out the real criminal."

"You may as well save your time and trouble, Mr. Stone. I am the man you seek, I freely confess my crime, and I accept my fate, whatever it be. Can I do more?"

"Yes; if you are telling the truth, go on, and relate details. What weapon did you use?"

"My own revolver."

"Where is it?"

"I threw it out of the window."

"Which window?"

"The—the bay window, in my den."

"In this room?"

"Yes."

"That window there?" Stone pointed to the big bay.

"Yes."

"You were sitting there at the time of the shot, were you not, Miss Wheeler?" Stone turned to Maida, who, white-faced and trembling, listened to her father's statements.

"I was sitting there before the shot," the girl returned, speaking in quiet, steady tones, though a red spot burned in either cheek. "And then, when Mr. Appleby threatened my father, I shot him myself. My father is untruthful for my sake. In his love for me he is trying to take my crime on himself. Oh, believe me, Mr. Stone! Others can testify that I said, long ago, that I could willingly kill Mr. Appleby. He has made my dear father's life a living grave! He has changed a brilliant, capable man of affairs to a sad and broken-hearted recluse. A man who had everything to live for, everything to interest and occupy his mind, was condemned to a solitary imprisonment, save for the company of his family! My father's career would have been notable, celebrated; but that Samuel Appleby put an end to fifteen years ago, for no reason but petty spite and mean revenge! I had never seen the man, save as a small child, and when I learned he was at last coming here, my primitive passions were stirred, my sense of justice awoke and my whole soul was absorbed in a wild impulse to rid the world of such a demon in human form! I told my parents I was capable of killing him; they reproved me, so I said no more. But I brooded over the project, and made ready, and then—when Mr. Appleby threatened my father, talked to him brutally, scathingly, fairly turning the iron in his soul—I could stand it no longer, and I shot him down as I would have killed a venomous serpent! I do not regret the act—though I do fear the consequences."

Maida almost collapsed, but pulled herself together, to add:

"That is the truth. You must disregard and disbelieve my father's noble efforts to save me by trying to pretend the crime was his own."

Stone looked at her pityingly. McGuire stared fixedly; the boy's eyes round with amazement at this outburst of self-condemnation.

Then Stone said, almost casually: "You, too, Mrs. Wheeler, confess to this crime, I believe."

"I am the real criminal," Sara Wheeler asserted, speaking very quietly but with a steady gaze into the eyes of the listening detective. "You can readily understand that my husband and daughter are trying to shield me, when I tell you that only I had opportunity. I had possessed myself of Mr. Wheeler's pistol and as I ran downstairs—well knowing the conversation that was going on, I shot through the doors as I passed and running on, threw the weapon far out into the shrubbery. It can doubtless be found. I must beg of you, Mr. Stone, that you thoroughly investigate these three stories, and I assure you you will find mine the true one, and the assertions of my husband and daughter merely loving but futile attempts to save me from the consequences of my act."

Fleming Stone smiled, a queer, tender little smile.

"It is certainly a new experience for me," he said, "when a whole family insist on being considered criminals. But I will reserve decision until I can look into matters a little more fully. Now, who can give me any information on the matter, outside of the identity of the criminal?"

Jeffrey Allen volunteered the story of the fire, and Keefe told of the strange bugle call that had been heard.

"You heard it, Mr. Keefe?" asked Stone, after listening to the account.

"No; I was with Mr. Appleby on a trip to Boston. I tell it as I heard the tale from the household here."

Whereupon the Wheeler family corroborated Keefe's story, and Fleming Stone listened attentively to the various repetitions.

"You find that bugler, and you've got your murderer," Curtis Keefe said, bluntly. "You agree, don't you, Mr. Stone, that it was no phantom who blew audible notes on a bugle?"

"I most certainly agree to that. I've heard many legends, in foreign countries, of ghostly drummers, buglers and bagpipers, but they are merely legends—I've never found anyone who really heard the sounds. And, moreover, those things aren't even legends in America. Any bugling done in this country is done by human lungs. Now, this bugler interests me. I think, with you, Mr. Keefe, that to know his identity would help us—whether he proves to be the criminal or not."

"He's the criminal," Keefe declared, again. "Forgive me, Mr. Stone, if my certainty seems to you presumptuous or forward, but I'm so thoroughly convinced of the innocence of the Wheeler family, that perhaps I am over enthusiastic in my theory."

"'A theory doesn't depend on enthusiasm," returned Stone, "but on evidence and proof. Now, how can we set about finding this mysterious bugler—whether phantom or human?"

"I thought that's what you're here to do," Sam Appleby said, looking helplessly at Fleming Stone.

"We are," piped up Terence McGuire, as Stone made no reply. "That's our business, and, consequentially, it shall be done."

The boy assumed an air of importance that was saved from being objectionable by his good-humored face and frank, serious eyes. "I'll just start in and get busy now," he went on, and rising, he bobbed a funny little bow that included all present, and left the room.

It was mid-afternoon, and as they looked out on the wide lawn they saw McGuire strolling slowly, hands in pockets and seemingly more absorbed in the birds and flowers than in his vaunted "business."

"Perhaps McGuire needs a little explanation," Stone smiled. "He is my right-hand man, and a great help in detail work. But he has a not altogether unearned reputation for untruthfulness. Indeed, his nickname is Fibsy, because of a congenital habit of telling fibs. I advise you of this, because I prefer you should not place implicit confidence in his statements."

"But, Mr. Stone," cried Maida, greatly interested, "how can he be of any help to you if you can't depend on what he says?"

"Oh, he doesn't lie to me," Stone assured her; "nor does he tell whoppers at any time. Only, it's his habit to shade the truth when it seems to him advisable. I do not defend this habit; in fact, I have persuaded him to stop it, to a degree. But you know how hard it is to reform entirely."

"It won't affect his usefulness, since he doesn't lie to his employer," Appleby said, "and, too, it's none of our business. I've engaged Mr. Stone to solve the mystery of my father's death, and I'm prepared to give him full powers. He may conduct his investigations on any plan he chooses. My only stipulation is that he shall find a criminal outside the Wheeler family."

"A difficult and somewhat unusual stipulation," remarked Stone,

"Why difficult?" Dan Wheeler said, quickly.

"Because, with three people confessing a crime, and no one else even remotely suspected, save a mysterious and perhaps mythical bugle-player, it does not seem an easy job to hunt up and then hunt down a slayer."

"But you'll do it," begged Appleby, almost pleadingly, "for it must be done."

"We'll see," Stone replied. "And now tell me more about the fire in the garage. It occurred at the time of the shooting, you say? What started it?"

But nobody knew what started it.

"How could we know?" asked Jeff Allen, "It was only a small fire and the most it burned was the robe in Mr. Appleby's own car and a motor coat that was also in the car."

"Whose coat?" asked Stone.

"Mine," said Keefe, ruefully. "A bit of bad luck, too, for it was a new one. I had to get another in place of it."

"And you think the fire was the result of a dropped cigarette or match by Mr. Appleby's chauffeur?"

"I don't know," returned Keefe. "He denies it, of course, but it must have been that or an incendiary act of some one."

"Maybe the bugler person," suggested Stone.

"Maybe," assented Keefe, though he did not look convinced.

"I think Mr. Keefe thinks it was the work of my own men," said Dan Wheeler. "And it may have been. There's one in my employ who has an ignorant, brutal spirit of revenge, and if he thought Samuel Appleby was inimical to me, he would be quite capable of setting fire to the Appleby car. That may be the fact of the case."

"It may be," agreed Stone. "Doubtless we can find out—"

"How?" asked Allen. "That would be magician's work, I think."

"A detective has to be a magician," Stone smiled at him. "We quite often do more astounding tricks than that."

"Go to it, then!" cried Appleby. "That's the talk I like to hear. Questions and answers any of us can put over. But the real detecting is like magic. At least, I can't see how it's done. Duff in, Mr. Stone. Get busy."

The group dispersed then, Fleming Stone going to his room and the others straying off by twos or threes.

Burden, who had said almost nothing during the confab, declared he wanted a talk with the great detective alone, and would await his pleasure.

So Burdon sat by himself, brooding, on the veranda, and presently saw the boy, Fibsy, returning toward the house.

"Come here, young one," Burdon called out.

"Nixy, old one," was the saucy retort.

"Why not?" in a conciliatory tone.

"'Cause you spoke disrespectful like. I'm a detective, you know."

"All right, old pal; come here, will you?"

Fibsy grinned and came, seating himself on a cushioned swing nearby.

"Whatcha want?" he demanded,

"Only a line o' talk. Your Mr. Stone, now, do you think he'll show up soon, or has he gone for a nap?"

"Fleming Stone doesn't take naps," Fibsy said, disdainfully; "he isn't that sort."

"Then he'll be down again shortly?"

"Dunno. Maybe he's begun his fasting and prayer over this phenomenal case."

"Does he do that?"

"How do I know? I'm not of a curious turn of mind, me havin' other sins to answer for."

"I know. Mr. Stone told us you have no respect for the truth."

"Did he, now! Well, he's some mistaken! I have such a profound respect for the truth that I never use it except on very special occasions."

"Is this one?"

"It is not! Don't believe a word I say just now. In fact, I'm so lit up with the beauties and glories of this place, that I hardly know what I am a-saying! Ain't it the show-place, though!"

"Yes, it is. Looky here, youngster, can't you go up and coax Mr. Stone to see me—just a few minutes?"

"Nope; can't do that. But you spill it to me, and if it's worth it, I'll repeat it to him. I'm really along for that very purpose, you see."

"But I haven't anything special to tell him—"

"Oh, I see! Just want the glory and honor of chinning with the great Stone!"

As this so nearly expressed Burdon's intention, he grinned sheepishly, and Fibsy understood.

"No go, old top," he assured him. "F. Stone will send for you if he thinks you'll interest him in the slightest degree. Better wait for the sending—it'll mean a more satisfactory interview all round."

"Well, then, let's you and me chat a bit."

"Oho, coming round to sort of like me, are you? Well, I'm willing. Tell me this: how far from the victim did the shooter stand?"

"The doctor said, as nearly as he could judge, about ten feet or so away."

"H'm," and Fibsy looked thoughtful. "That would just about suit all three of the present claimants for the honor, wouldn't it?"

"Yes; and would preclude anybody not inside the room."

"Unless he was close to the window."

"Sure. But it ain't likely, is it now, that a rank outsider would come right up to the window and fire through it, and not be seen by anybody?"

"No; it isn't. And, of course, if that had happened, and any one of the three Wheelers had seen it, they would be only too glad to tell of it. I wonder they haven't made up some such yarn as that."

"You don't know the Wheelers. I do, and I can see how they would perjure themselves—any of them—and confess to a crime they didn't commit, to save each other—but it wouldn't occur to them to invent a murderer—or to say they saw some one they didn't see. Do you get the difference?"

"Being an expert in the lyin' game, I do," and Fibsy winked,

"It isn't only that. It's not only that they're unwilling to lie about it, but they haven't the—the, well, ingenuity to contrive a plausible yarn."

"Not being lying experts, just as I said," Fibsy observed. "Well, we all have our own kind of cleverness. Now, mine is finding things. Want to see an example?"

"Yes, I do."

"All right. How far did you say the shooter person stood from his victim?"

"About ten feet—but I daresay it might be two or three feet, more or less."

"No; they can judge closer'n that by the powder marks. The truth wouldn't vary more'n a foot or so, from their say. Now, s'posin' the shooter did throw the revolver out of the bay window, as the three Wheelers agree, severally, they did do, where would it most likely land?"

"In that clump of rhododendrons."

"Yep; if they threw it straight ahead. I s'pose you've looked there for it?"

"Yes, raked the place thoroughly."

"All right. Now if they slung the thing over toward the right, where would it land?"

"On the smooth lawn."

"And you didn't find it there!"

"No. What are you doing? Stringing me?"

"Oh, no, sir; oh, no! Now, once again. If they chanced to fling said revolver far to the left, where would it land?"

"Why—in that big bed of ferns—if they threw it far enough."

"Looked there?"

"No; I haven't."

"C'mon, let's take a squint."

Fibsy rose and lounged over toward the fern bed, Burdon following, almost certain he was being made game of.

Chapter 12: The Garage Fire

"Now, watch me," he said, and with a quick thrust of his arm down among the ferns, he drew forth a revolver, which he turned over to Burdon.

"Land o' goodness!" exclaimed that worthy. "Howja know it was there?"

"Knew it must be—looked for it—saw it," returned the boy, nonchalantly, and then, hearing a short, sharp whistle, he looked up at the house to see Fleming Stone regarding him from an upper window.

"Found the weapon, Fibs?" he inquired.

"Yes, Mr. Stone."

"All right. Bring it up here, and ask Mr. Burdon to come along."

Delighted at the summons, Burdon followed the boy's flying feet and they went up to Stone's rooms. A small and pleasant sitting-room had been given over to the detective, and he admitted his two visitors, then closed the door.

"Doing the spectacular, Terence?" Stone said, smiling a little.

"Just one grandstand play," the boy confessed. As a matter of fact, he had located the pistol sometime earlier, but waited to make the discovery seem sensational.

"All right; let's take a look at it."

Without hesitation, Burdon pronounced the revolver Mr. Wheeler's. It had no initials on it, but from Wheeler's minute description, Burdon recognized it beyond reasonable doubt. One bullet had been fired from it, and the calibre corresponded to the shot that had killed Samuel Appleby.

"Oh, it's the right gun, all right," Burdon said, "but I never thought of looking over that way for it. Must have been thrown by a left-handed man."

"Oh, not necessarily," said Stone. "But it was thrown with a conscious desire to hide it, and not flung away in a careless or preoccupied moment."

"And what do you deduce from that?" asked Burdon, quite prepared to hear the description of the murderer's physical appearance and mental attainments.

"Nothing very definite," Stone mused. "We might say it looked more like the act of a strong-willed man such as Mr. Wheeler, than of a frightened and nervously agitated woman."

"If either of those two women did it," Burdon offered, "she wasn't nervous or agitated. They're not that sort. They may go to pieces afterward, but whatever Mrs. Wheeler or Maida undertake to do, they put it over all right. I've known 'em for years, and I never knew either of them to show the white feather."

"Well, it was not much of an indication, anyway," Stone admitted, "but it does prove a steady nerve and a planning brain that would realize the advisability of flinging the weapon where it would not be probably sought. Now, as this is Mr. Wheeler's revolver, there's no use asking the three suspects anything about it. For each has declared he or she used it and flung it away. That in itself is odd—I mean that they should all tell the same story. It suggests not collusion so much as the idea that whoever did the shooting was seen by one or both of the others."

"Then you believe it was one of the three Wheelers?" asked Burdon.

"I don't say that, yet," returned Stone. "But they must be reckoned with. I want to eliminate the innocent two and put the guilt on the third—if that is where it belongs."

"And if not, which way are you looking?"

"Toward the fire. That most opportune fire in the garage seems to me indicative of a criminal who wanted to create a panic so he could carry out his murderous design with neatness and despatch."

"And that lets out the women?"

"Not if, as you say, they're of the daring and capable sort."

"Oh, they are! If Maida Wheeler did this thing, she could stage the fire easily enough. Or Mrs. Wheeler could, either. They're hummers when it comes to efficiency and actually doing things!"

"You surprise me. Mrs. Wheeler seems such a gentle, delicate personality."

"Yep; till she's roused. Then she's full of tiger! Oh, I know Sara Wheeler. You ask my wife what Mrs. Wheeler can do!"

"Tell me a little more of this conditional pardon matter. Is it possible that for fifteen years Mr. Wheeler has never stepped over to the forbidden side of his own house?"

"Perfectly true. But it isn't his house, it's Mrs. Wheeler's. Her folks are connected with the Applebys and it was the work of old Appleby that the property came to Sara with that tag attached, that she must live in Massachusetts. Also, Appleby pardoned Wheeler on condition that he never stepped foot into Massachusetts. And there they were. It was Sara Wheeler's ingenuity and determination that planned the house on the state line, and she has seen to it that Dan Wheeler never broke parole. It's second nature to him now, of course."

"But I'm told that he did step over the night of the murder. That he went into the sitting-room of his wife— or maybe into the forbidden end of that long living-room—to see the fire. It would be a most natural thing for him to do."

"Not natural, no, sir." Burdon rubbed his brow thoughtfully. "Yet he might 'a' done it. But one misstep like that ought to be overlooked, I think."

"And would be by his friends—but suppose there's an enemy at work. Suppose, just as a theory, that somebody is ready to take advantage of the peculiar situation, that seems to prove Dan Wheeler was either outside his prescribed territory—or he was the murderer. To my way of thinking, at present, that man's alibi is his absence from the scene of the crime. And, if he was absent, he must have been over the line. I know this from talks I've had with the servants and the family and guests, and I'm pretty confident that Wheeler was either in the den or in the forbidden north part of the house at the moment of the murder."

"Why don't you know which it was?" asked Burdon, bluntly.

"Because," said Stone, not resenting the question, "because I can't place any dependence on the truth of the family's statements. For three respectable, God-fearing citizens, they are most astonishingly willing, even eager, to perjure themselves. Of course, I know they do it for one another's sake. They have a strange conscience that allows them to lie outright for the sake of a loved one. And, it may be, commit murder for the sake of a loved one! But all this I shall straighten out when I get further along. The case is so widespread, so full of ramifications and possible side issues, I have to go carefully at first, and not get entangled in false clues."

"Got any clue, sir? Any real ones?"

"Meaning dropped handkerchiefs and broken cuff-links?" Stone chaffed him. "Well, there's the pistol. That's a material clue. But, no, I can't produce anything else—at present. Well, Terence, what luck?"

Fibsy, who had slipped from the room at the very beginning of this interview, now returned.

"It's puzzlin'—that's what it is, puzzlin'," he declared, throwing himself astride of a chair. "I've raked that old garage fore and aft, but I can't track down the startings of that fire. You see, the place is stucco and all that, and besides the discipline of this whole layout is along the lines of p'ison neatness! Everybody that works at Sycamore Ridge has to be a very old maid for keeping things clean! So, there's no chance for accumulated rubbish or old rags or spontaneous combustion or anything of the sort. Nextly, none of the three men who have any call to go into the garage ever smoke in there. That's a Mede and Persian law. Gee, Mr. Wheeler is some efficient boss! Well, anyway, after the fire, though they tried every way to find out what started it, they couldn't find a thing! There was no explanation but a brand dropped from the skies, or a stroke of lightning! And there was no storm on. It wouldn't all be so sure, but the morning after, it seems, Mr. Allen and Mr. Keefe were doin' some sleuthin' on their own, and they couldn't find out how the fire started. So, they put it up to the garage men, and they hunted, too. It seems nothing was burnt but some things in Mr. Appleby's car, which, of course, lets out his chauffeur, who had no call to burn up his own duds. And a coat of his was burned and also a coat of Mr. Keefe's."

"What were those coats doing in an unused car?" asked Stone.

"Oh, they were extra motor coats, or raincoats, or something like that, and they always staid in the car."

"Where, in the car?"

"I asked that," Fibsy returned, "and they were hanging on the coat-rail. I thought there might have been matches in the pockets, but they say no. There never had been matches in those coat pockets, nor any matches in the Appleby car, for that matter."

"Well, the fire is pretty well mixed up in the murder," declared Stone. "Now it's up to us to find out how."

"Ex-cuse me, Mr. Stone," and Burdon shook his head; "you'll never get at it that way."

"Ex-cuse me, Mr. Burdon," Fibsy flared back, "Mr. Stone will get at it that way, if he thinks that's the way to look. You don't know F. Stone yet—"

"Hush up, Fibs; Mr. Burdon will know if I succeed, and, perhaps he's right as to the unimportance of the fire, after all."

"You see," Burden went on, unabashed, "Mr. Keefe—now, he's some smart in the detective line—he said, find your phantom bugler, and you've got your murderer! Now, what nonsense that is! As if a marauding villain would announce himself by playing on a bugle!"

"Yet there may be something in it," demurred Stone. "It may well be that the dramatic mind that staged this whole mysterious affair is responsible for the bugle call, the fire, and the final crime."

"In that case, it's one of the women," Burdon said. "They could do all that, either of them, if they wanted to; but Dan Wheeler, while he could kill a man on provocation—it would be an impulsive act—not a premeditated one. No, sir! Wheeler could see red, and go Berserk, but he couldn't plan out a complicated affair like you're turning this case into!"

"I'm not turning it into anything," Stone laughed. "I'm taking it as it is presented to me, but I do hold that the phantom bugler and the opportune fire are theatrical elements."

"A theatrical element, too, is the big sycamore," and Burdon smiled. "Now, if that tree should take a notion to walk over into Massachusetts, it would help out some."

"What's that?" cried Fibsy. "What do you mean?"

"Well, the Wheelers have got a letter from Appleby, written while he was still governor, and it says that when the big sycamore goes into Massachusetts, Wheeler can go, too. But it can't be done by a trick. I mean, they can't transplant the thing, or chop it down and take the wood over. It's got to go of its own accord."

"Mere teasing," said Stone.

"Yes, sir, just that. Appleby had a great streak of teasing. He used to tease everybody just for the fun of seeing them squirm. This whole Wheeler business was the outcome of Appleby's distorted love of fun. And

Wheeler took it so seriously that Appleby kept it up. I'll warrant, if Wheeler had treated the whole thing as a joke, Appleby would have let up on him. But Dan Wheeler is a solemn old chap, and he saw no fun in the whole matter."

"I don't blame him," commented Stone. "Won't he get pardoned now?"

"No, sir, he won't. Some folks think he will, but I know better. The present governor isn't much for pardoning old sentences—he says it establishes precedent and all that. And the next governor is more than likely to say the same."

"I hear young Mr. Appleby isn't going to run."

"No, sir, he ain't. Though I daresay he will some other time. But this death of his father and the mystery and all, is no sort of help to a campaign. And, too, young Appleby hasn't the necessary qualifications to conduct a campaign, however good he might be as governor after he got elected. No; Sam won't run."

"Who will?"

"Dunno, I'm sure. But there'll be lots ready and eager for a try at it."

"I suppose so. Well, Burdon, I'm going down now to ask some questions of the servants. You know they're a mine of information usually."

"Kin I go?" asked Fibsy.

"Not now, son. You stay here, or do what you like. But don't say much and don't antagonize anybody."

"Not me, F. Stone!"

"Well, don't shock anybody, then. Behave like a gentleman and a scholar."

"Yessir," Fibsy ducked a comical bow, and Burdon, understanding he was dismissed, went home.

To the dining-room Stone made his way, and asked a maid there if he might see the cook.

Greatly frightened, the waitress brought the cook to the dining-room.

But the newcomer, a typical, strong-armed, strong-minded individual, was not at all abashed.

"What is it you do be wantin", sor?" she asked, civilly enough, but a trifle sullenly.

"Only a few answers to direct questions. Where were you when you first heard the alarm of the garage fire?"

"I was in me kitchen, cleanin' up after dinner."

"What did, you do?"

"I ran out the kitchen door and, seein' flames, I ran toward the garage."

"Before you ran, you were at the rear of the house—I mean the south side, weren't you?"

"Yes, sor, I was."

"You passed along the south veranda?"

"Not along it," the cook looked at him wonderingly—" but by the end of it, like."

"And did you see any one on the veranda? Any one at all?"

The woman thought hard. "Well, I sh'd have said no—first off—but now you speak of it, I must say I do have a remimbrance of seein' a figger—but sort of vague like."

"You mean your memory of it is vague—you don't mean a shadowy figure?"

"No, sor. I mean I can't mind it rightly, now, for I was thinkin' intirely of the fire, and so as I was runnin' past the end of the verandy all I can say is, I just glimpsed like, a person standin' there."

"Standing?"

"Well, he might have been moving—I dunno."

"Are you sure it was a man?"

"I'm not. I'm thinkin' it was, but yet, I couldn't speak it for sure."

"Then you went on to the fire?"

"Yes, sor."

"And thought no more about the person on the veranda?"

"No, sor. And it niver wud have entered me head again, savin' your speakin' of it now. Why—was it the—the man that—"

"Oh, probably not. But everything I can learn is of help in discovering the criminal and perhaps freeing your employers from suspicion."

"And I wish that might be! To put it on the good man, now! And worse, upon the ladies—angels, both of them!"

"You are fond of the family, then?"

"I am that! I've worked here for eight years, and never a cross word from the missus or the master. As for Miss Maida—she's my darlint."

"They're fortunate in having you here," said Stone, kindly. "That's all, now, cook, unless you can remember anything more of that person you saw."

"Nothin' more, sor. If I do, I'll tell you."

Thinking hard, Stone left her.

It was the most unusual case he had ever attempted. If he looked no further for the murderer than the Wheeler family, he still had enough to do in deciding which one of the three was guilty. But he yearned for another suspect. Not a foolish phantom that went around piping, or a perhaps imaginary prowler stalking on the piazza., but a real suspect with a sound, plausible motive.

Though, to be sure, the Wheelers had motive enough. To be condemned to an absurd restriction and then teased about it, was enough to make life gall and wormwood to a sensitive man like Wheeler.

And who could say what words had passed between them at that final interview? Perhaps Appleby had goaded him to the breaking point; perhaps Wheeler had stood it, but his wife, descending the stairs and hearing the men talk, had grown desperate at last; or, and Stone knew he thought this most plausible of all, perhaps Maida, in her window-seat, had stood as long as she could the aspersions and tauntings directed at her adored father, and had, with a reckless disregard of consequences, silenced the enemy forever.

Of young Allen, Stone had no slightest suspicion. To be sure, his interests were one with the Wheeler family, and moreover, he had hoped for a release from restrictions that would let the Wheelers go into Massachusetts and thereby make possible his home there with Maida.

For Maida's vow that she would never go into the state if her father could not go, too, was, Allen knew, inviolable.

All this Stone mulled over, yet had no thought that Allen was the one he was seeking. Also, Curtis Keefe had testified that Allen was with him at the fire, during the time that included the moment of shooting.

Strolling out into the gardens, the detective made his way to the great tree, the big sycamore.

Here Fibsy joined him, and at Stone's tacit nod of permission, the boy sat down beside his superior on the bench under the tree.

"What's this about the tree going to Massachusetts?" Fibsy asked, his freckled face earnestly inquiring.

"One of old Appleby's jokes," Stone returned. "Doubtless made just after a reading of 'Macbeth.' You know, or if you don't, you must read it up for yourself, there's a scene there that hinges on Birnam Wood going to Dunsinane. I can't take time to tell you about it, but quite evidently it pleased the old wag to tell Mr. Wheeler that he could go into his native state when this great tree went there."

"Meaning not at all, I s'pose."

"Of course. And any human intervention was not allowed. So though Birnam Wood was brought to Dunsinane, such a trick is not permissible in his case. However, that's beside the point just now. Have you seen any of the servants?"

"Some. But I got nothing. They're willing enough to talk, but they don't know anything. They say I'd better tackle the ladies' maid, a fair Rachel. So I'm going for her. But I bet I won't strike pay-dirt."

"You may. Skip along, now, for here comes Miss Maida, and she's probably looking for me."

Fibsy departed, and Maida, looking relieved to find Stone alone, came quickly toward him.

"You see, Mr. Stone," she began, "you must start straight in this thing. And the only start possible is for you to be convinced that I killed Mr. Appleby."

"But you must admit, Miss Wheeler, that I am not too absurd in thinking that though you say you did it, you are saying it to shield some one else—some one who is near and dear to you."

"I know you think that—but it isn't so. How can I convince you?"

"Only by circumstantial evidence. Let me question you a bit. Where did you get the revolver?"

"From my father's desk drawer, where he always keeps it."

"You are familiar with firearms?"

"My father taught me to shoot years ago. I'm not a crack shot—but that was not necessary."

"You premeditated the deed?"

"For some time I have felt that I wanted to kill that man."

"Your conscience?"

"Is very active. I deliberately went against its dictates for my father's sake."

"And you killed Mr. Appleby because he hounded your father in addition to the long deprivation he had imposed on him?"

"No, not that alone. Oh, I don't want to tell you—but, if you won't believe me otherwise, Mr. Stone, I will admit that I had a new motive—"

"A new one?"

"Yes, a secret that I learned only a day or so before—before Mr. Appleby's death."

"The secret was Appleby's?"

"Yes; that is, he knew it. He told it to me. If any one else should know it, it would mean the utter ruin and desolation of the lives of my parents, compared to which this present condition of living is Paradise itself!"

"This is true, Miss Wheeler?"

"Absolutely true. Now, do you understand why I killed him?"

CHAPTER 13: SARA WHEELER

Fleming Stone was deeply interested in the Appleby case.

While his logical brain could see no possible way to look save toward one of the three Wheelers, yet his soul revolted at the thought that any one of them was the criminal.

Stone was well aware of the fact that the least seemingly guilty often proved to be a deep-dyed villain, yet he hesitated to think that Dan Wheeler had killed his old enemy, and he could not believe it was a woman's work. He was impressed by Maida's story, especially by the fact that a recent development had made her more strongly desirous to be rid of old Appleby. He wondered if it did not have something to do with young Appleby's desire to marry her, and determined to persuade her to confide further in him regarding the secret she mentioned.

But first, he decided to interview Mrs. Wheeler. This could not be done offhand, so he waited a convenient season, and asked for a conference when he felt sure it would be granted.

Sara Wheeler received the detective in her sitting-room, and her manner was calm and collected as she asked him to make the interview as brief as possible.

"You are not well, Mrs. Wheeler?" Stone asked, courteously.

"I am not ill, Mr. Stone, but naturally these dreadful days have upset me, and the horror and suspense are still hanging over me. Can you not bring matters to a crisis? Anything would be better than present conditions!"

"If some member of your family would tell me the truth," Stone said frankly, "it would help a great deal.

You know, Mrs. Wheeler, when three people insist on being regarded as the criminal, it's difficult to choose among them. Now, won't you, at least, admit that you didn't shoot Mr. Appleby?"

"But I did," and the serene eyes looked at Stone calmly.

"Can you prove it—I mean, to my satisfaction? Tell me this: where did you get a pistol?"

"I used Mr. Wheeler's revolver."

"Where did you get it?"

"From the drawer in his desk, where he always keeps it."

Stone sighed. Of course, both Maida and her mother knew where the revolver was kept, so this was no test of their veracity as to the crime.

"When did you take it from the drawer?"

Sara Wheeler hesitated for an instant and from that, Stone knew that she had to think before she spoke. Had she been telling the truth, he argued, she would have answered at once.

But immediately she spoke, though with a shade of hesitation.

"I took it earlier in the day—I had it up in my own room."

"Yes; where did you conceal it there?"

"In—in a dresser drawer."

"And, when you heard the alarm of fire, you ran downstairs in consequence—but you paused to get the revolver and take it with you!"

This sounded absurd, but Sara Wheeler could see no way out of it, so she assented.

"Feeling sure that you would find your husband and Mr. Appleby in such a desperate quarrel that you would be called upon to shoot?"

"I—I overheard the quarrel from upstairs," she faltered, her eyes piteous now with a baffled despair.

"Then you went down because of the quarreling voices—not because of the fire-alarm?"

Unable to meet Stone's inexorable gaze, Mrs. Wheeler's eyes fell and she nervously responded: "Well, it was both."

"Now, see here," Stone said, kindly; "you want to do anything you can, don't you, to help your husband and daughter?"

"Yes, of course!" and the wide-open eyes now looked at him hopefully.

"Then will you trust me far enough to believe that I think you will best help them by telling the truth?"

"Oh, I can't!" and with a low moan the distracted woman hid her face in her hands.

"Please do; your attitude proves you are concealing important information. I am more than ever sure you are not the guilty one—and I am not at all sure that it was either of the other two."

"Then who could it have been?" and Sara Wheeler looked amazed.

"That we don't know. If I had a hint of any direction to look I'd be glad. But if you will shed what light you can, it may be of great help."

"Even if it seems to incriminate my—"

"What can incriminate them more than their own confessions?"

"Their confessions contradict each other. They can't both be guilty."

"And you don't know which one is?"

"N-no," came the faltering reply.

"But that admission contradicts your own confession. Come now, Mrs. Wheeler, own up to me that you didn't do it, and I'll not tell any one else, unless it becomes necessary."

"I will tell you, for I can't bear this burden alone any longer! I did go downstairs because of the alarm of fire, Mr. Stone. Just before I came to the open door of the den, I heard a shot, and as I passed the door of the den, I saw Mr. Appleby, fallen slightly forward in his chair, my

husband standing at a little distance looking at him, and
Maida in the bay window, also staring at them both.

"What did you do? Go in?"

"No; I was so bewildered, I scarcely knew which way
to turn, and in my fear and horror I ran into my own
sitting-room and fell on the couch there in sheer collapse."

"You stayed there?"

"Until I heard voices in the den—the men came back
from the fire and discovered the—the tragedy. At least, I
think that's the way it was. It's all mixed up in my mind.
Usually I'm very clear-headed and strong nerved, but
that scene seemed to take away all my will-power—all my
vitality."

"I don't wonder. What did you do or say?"

"I had a vague fear that my husband or daughter
would be accused of the crime, and so, at once, I declared
it was the work of the phantom bugler. You've heard
about him?"

"Yes. You didn't think it was he, though, did you?"

"I wanted to—yes, I think I did. You see, I don't think
the bugler was a phantom, but I do think he was a
criminal. I mean, I think it was somebody who meant
harm to my husband. I—well—I think maybe the shot
was meant for Mr. Wheeler."

Stone looked at her sharply, and said: "Please, Mrs.
Wheeler, be honest with me, whatever you may pretend
to others. Are you not springing that theory in a further
attempt to direct suspicion away from Mr. Wheeler?"

She gave a gesture of helplessness. "I see I can hide
nothing from you, Mr. Stone! You are right—but may
there not be a chance that it is a true theory after all?"

"Possibly; if we can find any hint of the bugler's
identity. Mr. Keefe says, find the bugler and you've found
the murderer."

"I know he does, but Keefe is—as I am—very anxious
to direct suspicion away from the Wheeler family. You
see, Mr. Keefe is in love with my daughter—"

"As who isn't? All the young men fall down before her charms!"

"It is so. Although she is engaged to Mr. Allen, both Mr. Keefe and Mr. Sam Appleby are hopeful of yet winning her regard. To me it is not surprising, for I think Maida the very flower of lovely girlhood, but I also think those men should recognize Jeffrey Allen's rights and cease paying Maida such definite attentions."

"It is hard to repress an ardent admirer," Stone admitted, "and as you say, that is probably Keefe's intent in insisting on the finding of the bugler. You do not, then, believe in your old legend?"

"I do and I don't. My mind has a tendency to revere and love the old traditions of my family, but when it comes to real belief I can't say I am willing to stand by them. Yet where else can we look for a criminal—other than my own people?"

"Please tell me just what you saw when you looked into the den immediately after you heard the shot. You must realize how important this testimony is."

"I do," was the solemn reply. "I saw, as I told you, both my husband and my daughter looking at Mr. Appleby as he sat in his chair. I did not know then that he was dead, but he must have been dead or dying. The doctors said the death was practically instantaneous."

"And from their attitude or their facial expression could you assume either your husband or daughter to have been the guilty one?"

"I can only say they both looked stunned and horrified. Just as one would expect them to look on the occasion of witnessing a horrible tragedy."

"Whether they were responsible for it or not?"

"Yes. But I'm not sure the attitude would have been different in the case of a criminal or a witness. I mean the fright and horror I saw on their faces would be the same if they had committed a crime or had seen it done."

Stone considered this. "You may be right," he said; "I daresay absolute horror would fill the soul in either case, and would produce much the same effect in appearance. Now, let us suppose for a moment, that one or other of the two did do the shooting—wait a moment!" as Mrs. Wheeler swayed uncertainly in her chair. "Don't faint. I'm supposing this only in the interests of you and yours. Suppose, I say, that either Mr. Wheeler or Miss Wheeler had fired the weapon—as they have both confessed to doing—which would you assume, from their appearance, had done it?"

Controlling herself by a strong effort, Sara Wheeler answered steadily, "I could not say. Honestly, to my startled eyes they seemed equally horrified and stunned."

"Of course they would. You see, Mrs. Wheeler, the fact that they both confess it, makes it look as if one of them did do it, and the other having witnessed the deed, takes over the blame to save the guilty one. This sounds harsh, but we have to face the facts. Then, if we can get more or different facts, so much the better."

"You're suggesting, then, that one of my people did do it, and the other saw it done?"

"I'm suggesting that that might be the truth, and so far as we can see now, is the most apparent solution. But I'm not saying it is the truth, nor shall I relax my efforts to find another answer to our problem. And I want to tell you that you have helped materially by withdrawing your own confession. Every step I can take toward the truth is helpful. You have lessened the suspects from three to two; now if I can eliminate another we will have but one; and if I can clear that one, we shall have to look elsewhere."

"That is specious argument, Mr. Stone," and Sara Wheeler fixed her large, sad eyes upon his face.

"For, if you succeeded in elimination of one of the two, it may be you cannot eliminate the third—and then—"

"And then your loving perjuries will be useless. True, but I must do my duty—and that means my duty to you all. I may tell you that Mr. Appleby, who employed me, asked me to find a criminal outside of your family, whether the real one or not."

"He put it that way!"

"He did; and while I do want to find the outside criminal, I can't find him if he doesn't exist."

"Of course not. I daresay I shall regret what I've told you, but—"

"But you couldn't help it, I know. Don't worry, Mrs. Wheeler. If you've no great faith in me, try to have a hopeful trust, and I assure you I will not betray it."

"Well, Mr. McGuire," Stone said to his adoring satellite, a little later, "there's one out."

"Mother Wheeler?"

"Yes, you young scamp; how did you know?"

"Saw you hobnobbing with her—she being took with a sudden attack of the confidentials—and, anyhow, two of 'em—at least—has got to cave in. You can ferret out which of 'em is George Washingtons and which isn't."

"Well, here's the way it seems to stand now. Mind, I only say seems to stand."

"Yessir."

"The father and daughter—both of whom confess to the shooting, were seen in the room immediately after the event. Now, they were on opposite sides of the room, the victim being about midway between them. Consequently, if one shot, the other was witness thereto. And, owing to the deep devotion obtaining between them, either father or daughter would confess to the crime to save the other."

"Then," Fibsy summed up, "Mr. Wheeler and Maida don't suspect each other; one did it, and both know which one."

"Well put. Now, which is which?"

"More likely the girl did the shooting. She's awful impulsive, awful high strung and awful fond of her father. Say the old Appleby gentleman was beratin' and oratin' and iratin' against Friend Wheeler, and say he went a leetle too far for Miss Maida to stand, and say she had that new secret, or whatever it is that's eatin' her— well, it wouldn't surprise me overly, if she up and shot the varmint."

"Having held the pistol in readiness?"

"Not nec'ess'rily. She coulda sprung across the room, lifted the weapon from its 'customed place in the drawer, and fired, all in a fleetin' instant o' time. And she's the girl to do it! That Maida, now, she could do anything! And she loves the old man enough to do anything. Touch and go—that's what she is! Especially go!"

"Well, all right. Yet, maybe it was the other way. Maybe, Wheeler, at the end of his patience, and knowing the 'secret,' whatever it may be, flung away discretion and grabbed up his own pistol and fired."

"Coulda been, F. Stone. Coulda been—easily. But—I lean to the Maida theory. Maida for mine, first, last, and all the time."

"For an admirer of hers, and you're not by yourself in that, you seem cheerfully willing to subscribe to her guilt."

"Well, I ain't! But I do want to get the truth as to the three Wheelers. And once I get it fastened on the lovely Maida, I'll set to work to get it off again. But, I'll know where I'm at."

"And suppose we fasten it on the lovely Daniel?"

"That's a serious proposition, F. Stone. For, if he did it, he did it. And if Maida did it—she didn't do it. See?"

"Not very clearly; but never mind, you needn't expound. It doesn't interest me."

Fibsy looked comically chagrined, as he often did when Stone scorned his ideas, but he said nothing except:

"Orders, sir?"

"Yes, Terence. Hunt up Rachel, the maid, and find out all she knows. Use your phenomenal powers of enchantment and make her come across."

"'Tis the same as done, sir!" declared the boy, and he departed at once in search of Rachel.

He sauntered out of the north door and took a roundabout way to the kitchen quarters.

Finally he found the cook, and putting on his best and most endearing little boy effects, he appealed for something to eat.

"Not but what I'm well treated at the table," he said, "but, you know what boys are."

"I do that," and the good-natured woman furnished him with liberal pieces of pie and cake.

"Great," said Fibsy, eating the last crumb as he guilefully complimented her culinary skill, "and now I've got to find a person name o' Rachel. Where might she be?"

"She might be 'most anywhere, but she isn't anywhere," was the cryptic reply.

"Why for?"

"Well, she's plain disappeared, if you know what that means."

"Vamoosed? Skipped? Faded? Slid? Oozed out?"

"Yes; all those. Anyway, she isn't on the place."

"Since when?"

"Why, I saw her last about two hours ago. Then when Mrs. Wheeler wanted her she wasn't to be found."

"And hasn't sence ben sane?"

"Just so. And as you are part and parcel of that detective layout that's infestin' the house an' grounds, I wish you'd find the hussy."

"Why, why, what langwitch! Why call her names?"

"She's a caution! Get along now, and if you can't find her, at least you can quit botherin' me."

"All right. But tell me this, before we part. Did she confide to your willin' ears anything about the murder?"

"Uncanny you are, lad! How'd you guess it?"

"I'm a limb of Satan. What did she tell you? and when?"

"Only this morning; early, before she flew off."

"Couldn't very well have told you after she started."

"No impidence now. Well, she told me that the night of the murder, as she ran from here to the garage, she saw on the south veranda a man with a bugle pipe!"

"A pipe dream!"

"I dunno. But she told it like gospel truth."

"Just what did she say?"

"Said she saw a man—a live man, no phantom foolishness, on the south veranda, and he carried a bugle."

"Did he play on it?"

"No; just carried it like. But she says he musta been the murderer, and by the same token it's the man I saw!"

"Oho, you saw him, too?"

"As I told your master, I saw him, but not plain, as I ran along to the fire. Rachel, now, she saw him plain, so he musta been there. Well, belike, he was the murderer, and that sets my people free."

"Important if true, but are you both sure? And why, oh, why does the valuable Rachel choose this time to vanish? Won't she come back?"

"Who knows? She didn't take any luggage—"

"How did she go?"

"Nobody knows. She walked, of course—"

"Then she couldn't have gone far."

"Oh, well, she could walk to the railway station. It's only a fairish tramp. But why did she go?"

"I ask you why."

"And I don't know. But I suppose it was because she didn't want to be questioned about the man who shot."

"What! You didn't say she saw him shoot!"

"Yes, I did. Or I meant to. Anyway that's what Rachel said. The man with the bugle shot through the window and that's what killed Mr. Appleby."

"Oh, come now, this is too big a yarn to be true, especially when the yarner lights out at once after telling it!"

"Well, Rachel has her faults, but I never knew her to lie. And if it was the man I saw—why, that proves, at least, there was a man there."

"But you didn't see him clearly."

"But I saw him."

"Then he must be reckoned with. Now, Cookie, dear, we must find Rachel. We must! Do you hear? You help me and I bet we'll get her."

"But I've no idea where she went—"

"Of course you haven't. But think; has she any friends or relatives nearby?"

"Not one."

"Are there any trains about the time she left?"

"I don't know what time she left, but there's been no train since nine-thirty, and I doubt she was in time for that."

"She took no luggage?"

"No, I'll vouch for that."

"Then she's likely in the neighborhood. Is there any inn or place she could get a room and board?"

"Oh, land, she hasn't gone away to stay. She's scart at something most likely, and she'll be back by nightfall."

"She may and she may not. She must be found. Wait, has she a lover?"

"Well, they do say Fulton, the chauffeur, is sweet on her, but I never noticed it much."

"Who said he was?"

"Mostly she said it herself."

"She ought to know! Me for Fulton. Goodbye, Cookie, for the nonce," and waving a smiling farewell, Fibsy went off toward the garage.

CHAPTER 14: RACHEL'S STORY

"Hello, Fult," Fibsy sang out gaily to the chauffeur, and received a pleasant response, for few could resist the contagious smile of the round, freckled face of the boy.

"Hello, Mr. Fibsy," the other returned, "how you getting on with your detective work?"

"Fine; but I want a little help from you,"

"Me? I don't know anything about anything."

"Well, then tell me what you don't know. That fire now, here in the garage, the night of the murder, did you ever find out how it started?"

Fulton's face took on a perplexed look and he said: "No, we didn't—and it's a queer thing. It must have been started by some one purposely, for there's no way it could have come about by accident."

"Spontaneous combustion?"

"Whatever made you think of that? And it couldn't have been from old paint rags, or such, for there's nothing like that about. But—well, here's what I found."

Fulton produced a small bottle. It was empty and had no label or stopper, and Fibsy looked at it blankly.

"What is it?" he asked.

"Never see one like it?"

"No; have you?"

"Yes, I have. I was in the war, and bottles like that contained acid which, when combined with another acid, caused spontaneous combustion."

"Combined—how?"

"Well, they used to saturate some cloth or old clothes with the other acid, and throw them about. Then, when the time came they threw a little bottle like that, filled with acid, and with only a paper stopper, in among the clothes. The acid slowly ate out the paper stopper, and then the two acids caused combustion. So, by the time the fire started, the man who was responsible for it was far away from the scene."

"Whew! And you think that happened here?"

"There's the bottle. The fire began in Mr. Appleby's car. Two coats and a rug were burned—now, mightn't they have been sprinkled with the other acid—"

"Of course that's what happened! Why haven't you told this before?"

"I only found the bottle this morning. It had been kicked under a bench, and the sweeper found it. Then I fell a-thinking, for it's the very same sort of bottle I saw used over there. Somebody who knew that trick did it."

"And whoever did it is either Mr. Appleby's murderer, or an accomplice."

"You think the two crimes are connected, then?"

"Haven't a doubt of it. You're a clever chap, Fulton, to dope this out—"

"Well, there was no other explanation. Anything else hinted at carelessness of my management of this place, and that hurt my pride, for I like to think this garage the pink of perfection as to cleanliness and order."

"Mr. Wheeler is fortunate in having such a man as you. Now, one more thing, Fulton; where is Rachel?"

"Rachel!"

"Yes, your blush gives you away. If you know where she is, tell me. If she's done nothing wrong it can do no harm to find her. If she has done anything wrong, she must be found."

"I don't know where she is, Mr. Fibsy—"

"Call me McGuire. And if you don't know where she is, you know something about her disappearance. When did she go away?"

"I saw her last night. She said nothing about going away, but she seemed nervous and worried, and I couldn't say anything to please her."

"Can't you form any idea of where she might have gone? Be frank, Fulton, for much depends on getting hold of that girl."

"I can only say I've no idea where she is, but she may communicate with me. In that case—"

"In that case, let me know at once," Fibsy commanded, and having learned all he could there, he went off to think up some other means of finding the lost Rachel.

Meantime Sam Appleby was taking his departure.

"I have to go," he said, in response to the Wheelers' invitation to tarry longer; "because Keefe is coming down to-morrow. One of us ought to be in father's office all the time now, there's so much to attend to."

"Why is Mr. Keefe coming here?" asked Maida.

"Mr. Stone wants to see him," Appleby informed her. "You know, Keefe is more or less of a detective himself, and Mr. Stone thinks he may be helpful in finding the criminal. Miss Lane is coming also, she begged to, mostly, I think, because she took such a liking to you."

"I liked her, too," returned Maida; "she's a funny girl but a sincere, thorough nature."

"Yes, she is. Well, they'll only stay over a day or two, I can't spare them longer. Of course, they may be of help to Mr. Stone, and they may not. But I don't want to miss a trick in this investigation. What a queer little chap that boy of Stone's is!"

"Fibsy?" and Maida smiled. "Yes, he's a case! And he's my devoted slave."

"As who isn't?" exclaimed Appleby. "Oh, Maida, do give me a little encouragement. After this awful business is all over, mayn't I come back with a hope that you'll smile on me?"

"Don't talk that way, Sam. You know I'm engaged to Jeffrey."

"Oh, no, you're not. I mean, it can be possible for you to change your mind. Girls are often engaged to several men before they marry."

"I'm not that sort," and Maida smiled a little sadly.

"Be that sort, then."

"You seem to forget that I may be openly accused of crime at any moment. And a crime that hits you pretty closely."

"Don't say such things, dear. Neither you nor any of your people are responsible for the dreadful thing that happened to father—or, if you are, I never want to know it. And I do want you, Maida dear—so much—"

"Hush, Sam; I won't listen to anything like that from you."

"Not now, but later on," he urged. "Tell me that I may come back, Maida dear."

"Of course you may come here, whenever you like, but I hold out no hope of the sort you ask for."

"I shall hope all the same. I'd die if I didn't! Good-bye, Maida, for this time."

He went away to the train, and later, came Keefe and Genevieve Lane.

"Oh," the girl cried, "I'm so glad to be back here again, Maida. My, but you're prettier than ever! If you'd only touch up those pale cheeks—just a little bit—here, let me—"

She opened her ever-ready vanity box, and was about to apply a touch of rouge, but Maida sprang away from her.

"No, no, Genevieve, I never use it."

"Silly girl! You don't deserve the beauty nature gave you, if you're not willing to help it along a little yourself! How do you do, Mrs. Wheeler and Mr. Wheeler?"

She greeted them prettily, and Keefe, too, exchanged greetings with the family.

"Anything being done?" he asked, finally. "Has Mr. Stone discovered anything of importance?"

"Nothing very definite, I fear," returned Daniel Wheeler. He spoke wearily, and almost despairingly. Anxiety and worry had aged him, even in the last few days. "I do hope, Keefe, that you can be of assistance. You have a keen eye for details, and may know or remember some points that escaped our notice."

"I'm hoping I can help," Keefe returned with a serious face. "Can I see Stone shortly?"

"Yes, now. Come along into the den, he's in here."

The two men went to the den, where Stone and Fibsy were in deep consultation.

"Very glad to see you, Mr. Keefe," Fleming Stone acknowledged the introduction. "This is McGuire, my young assistant. You may speak frankly before him."

"If I have anything to speak," said Keefe. "I don't really know anything I haven't told, but I may remind Mr. Wheeler of some points he has forgotten."

"Well, let's talk it all over," Stone suggested, and they did.

Keefe was greatly surprised and impressed by the story of the cook's having seen a man on the south veranda at the time of the shooting.

"But she didn't see him clearly," Fibsy added.

"Couldn't she describe him?"

"No; she didn't see him plain enough. But the maid, Rachel, told cook that she saw the man, too, and that he carried a bugle. Cook didn't see the bugle."

"Naturally not, if she only saw the man vaguely," said Wheeler. "But, it begins to look as if there must have been a man there and if so, he may have been the criminal."

"Let us hope," said Keefe, earnestly. "Now, can you find this man, Mr. Stone?"

"We've got to find him," Stone returned, "whether we can or not. It's really a baffling case. I think we've discovered the origin of the fire in the garage."

He told the story that Fibsy had learned from the chauffeur, and Keefe was greatly interested.

"What are the acids?" he asked.

"I don't know the exact names," Stone admitted, "but they are of just such powers as Fulton described, and the thing is plausible. Here's the bottle." He offered the little vial for inspection and Keefe looked at it with some curiosity.

"The theory being," he said, "that the murderer first arranged for a fire in our car—in Mr. Appleby's car—and then waited for the fire to come off as planned. Then, at the moment of greatest excitement, he, being probably the man the servants saw—shot through the bay window and killed Mr. Appleby. You were fortunate, Miss Maida, that you weren't hit first!"

"Oh, I was in no danger. I sat well back in the window-seat, and over to one side, out of range of a shot from outside. And, too, Mr. Keefe, I can scarcely discuss this matter of the shot from outside, as I am, myself, the confessed criminal."

"Confessing only to save me from suspicion," said her father, with an affectionate glance. "But it won't do any good, dear. I take the burden of the crime and I own up that I did it. This man on the veranda—if, indeed, there was such a one, may have been any of the men servants about the place, startled by the cry of fire, and running to assure himself of the safety of the house and family. He, doubtless, hesitates to divulge his identity lest he be suspected of shooting."

"That's all right," declared Fibsy, "but if it was one of your men, he'd own up by this time. He'd know he wouldn't be suspected of shooting Mr. Appleby. Why should he do it?"

"Why should anybody do it, except myself?" asked Dan Wheeler. "Not all the detectives in the world can find any one else with a motive and opportunity. The fact that both my wife and daughter tried to take the crime off my shoulders only makes me more determined to tell the truth."

"But you're not telling the truth, dad," and Maida looked at him. "You know I did it—you know I had threatened to do it—you know I felt I just could not stand Mr. Appleby's oppression of you another day! And so— and so, I—"

"Go on, Miss Wheeler," urged Stone, "and so you—what did you do?"

"I ran across the den to the drawer where father keeps his pistol; I took it and shot—then I ran back to the window-seat—"

"What did you do with the pistol?"

"Threw it out of the window."

"Toward the right or left?"

"Why, I don't know."

"Try to think. Stand up there now, and remember which way you flung it."

Reluctantly, Maida went to the bay window, and stood there thinking.

"I don't know," she said, at last. "I can't remember."

"It doesn't matter," said Keefe. "I think we can prove that it was none of the Wheelers, but there was a man, an intruder, on the veranda who shot. Even if we never find out his identity, we may prove that he was really there. Where is this maid who saw him clearly? Rachel—is that her name?"

"That's a pretty thing, too!" Fibsy spoke up. "She has flew the coop."

"Gone! Where?" Keefe showed his disappointment.

"Nobody knows where. She just simply lit out. Even her lover doesn't know where she is."

"Who is her lover?"

"Fulton, the chauffeur. He's just about crazy over her disappearance."

"Oh, she'll return," surmised Stone. "She became frightened at something and ran off. I think she'll come back. If not, we'll have to give chase. We must find her, as she's the principal witness of the man on the veranda. Cook is not so sure about him."

"Who could he have been?" Keefe said. "Doubtless some enemy of Mr. Appleby, in no way connected with the Wheelers."

"Probably," agreed Stone.

"We found the pistol, you know, Mr. Keefe," remarked Fibsy.

"You did! Well, you have made progress. Where was it?"

"In the fern bed, not far from the veranda railing."

"Just where the man would have thrown it!" exclaimed Keefe.

"Or where I threw it," put in Daniel Wheeler.

"I'd like to see the exact place it was found," Keefe said.

"Come on, I'll show you," offered Fibsy and the two started away together.

"Here you are," and Fibsy showed the bed of ferns, which, growing closely together, made a dense hiding place."

"A wonder you ever found it," said Keefe. "How'd you happen to?"

"Oh, I just snooped around till I came to it. I says to myself, 'Either the murderer flung it away or he didn't. If he did, why it must be somewheres,' and it was."

"I see; and does Mr. Stone think the finding of it here points to either of the Wheelers?"

"Not necess'rily. You see, if the man we're looking for did the shooting, he's the one who threw the pistol in this here fern bed. And, you know yourself, it's more likely a man threw this farther than a woman."

"Miss Wheeler is athletic."

"I know, but I'm convinced that Miss Wheeler didn't do the deed. Ain't you?"

"Oh, I can't think she did it, of course. But it's all very mysterious."

"Not mysterious a bit. It's hard sleddin', but there ain't much mystery about it. Why, look a-here... If either the father or daughter did it, they both know which one it was. Therefore, one is telling the truth and one isn't. It won't be hard to find out which is which, but F. Stone, he's trying to find some one that'll let the Wheelers both out."

"Oh, that's his idea? And a mighty good one. I'll help all I can. Of course, the thing to do is to trace the pistol."

"Oh, it was Mr. Wheeler's pistol, all right."

"It was!" Keefe looked dismayed. "Then how can we suspect an outsider?"

"Well, he could have stolen Mr. Wheeler's pistol for the purpose of casting suspicion on him."

"Yes; that's so. Now to find that Rachel."

"Oh, do find her," Maida cried, overhearing the remark as she and Genevieve crossed the lawn toward Keefe and Fibsy.

The lad had not yet seen Miss Lane and he frankly admired her at once. Perhaps a sympathetic chord was struck by the similarity of their natures. Perhaps they intuitively recognized each other's gay impudence, for they engaged in a clash of words that immediately made them friends.

"Maybe Rachel'd come back if she knew you were here," he said. "I'm sure she'd admire to wait on such a pretty lady."

"Just tell her that you saw me," Genevieve said, "and I'll be glad to have her back. She's a first-class ladies' maid."

"Oh, then she only waits on first-class ladies?"

"Yes; that's why she's so fond of me. Do hunt her up."

"Well, cutie, just for you, I'll do that same. Where shall I go to look for her?"

"How should I know? But you keep watch of Fulton, and I'll bet he gets some word from her."

"Yes, they're sweethearts. Now, how do sweethearts get word to each other? You ought to know all about sweethearting."

"I don't," said Genevieve, demurely.

"Pshaw, now, that's too bad. Want me to teach you?"

"Yes—if you don't mind."

"Saunter away with me, then," and the saucy boy led Miss Lane off for a stroll round the grounds.

"Honest, now, do you want to help?" he asked.

"Yes, I do," she asserted. "I'm downright fond of Maida, and though I know she didn't do it, yet she and her father will be suspected unless we can find this other person. And the only way to get a line on him, seems to be through Rachel. Why do you suppose she ran away?"

"Can't imagine. Don't see how she could get scared."

"No; what would scare her? I think she's at some neighbor's."

"Let's you and me go to all the neighbors and see."

"All right. We'll go in the Wheelers' little car. Fulton will take us."

"Don't we get permission?"

"Nixy. They might say no, by mistake for a yes. Come on—we'll just hook Jack."

To the garage they went and easily persuaded Fulton to take them around to some of the neighboring houses.

And at the third one they visited they found Rachel. A friend of hers was a maid there, and she had taken Rachel in for a few days.

"Why did you run off?" queried Fulton.

"Oh, I don't know," and Rachel shuddered. "It all got on my nerves. Who's over there now?"

"Just the family, and the detectives and Mr. Keefe," Fulton answered. "Will you come home?"

"She will," Fibsy answered for her. "She will get right into this car and go at once—in the name of the law!" he added sternly, as Rachel seemed undecided.

Fibsy often used this phrase, and, delivered in an awe-inspiring tone, it was usually effective.

Rachel did get into the car, and they returned to Sycamore Lodge in triumph.

"Good work, Fibs," Stone nodded his approval. "Now, Rachel, sit right down here on the veranda, and tell us about that man you saw."

The girl was clearly frightened and her voice trembled, but she tried to tell her story.

"There's nothing to fear," Curtis Keefe said, kindly. "Just tell slowly and simply the story of your seeing the man and then you may be excused."

She gave him a grateful look, and seemed to take courage,

"Well, I was passing the veranda—"

"Coming from where and going where?" interrupted Stone, speaking gently.

"Why, I—I was coming from the—the garage—"

"Where you had been talking to Fulton?"

"Yes, sir."

"All right, go on."

"And I was going—going to go up to Mrs. Wheeler's room. I thought she might want me. And as I went by the veranda, I saw the man. He was a big man, and he carried a bugle."

"He didn't blow on it?"

"No, sir. Just waved it about like."

"You didn't see that he had a pistol?"

"I—I couldn't say, sir."

"Of course you couldn't," said Keefe. "Men with pistols don't brandish them until they get ready to shoot."

"But you saw this man shoot?" went on Stone.

"Yes, sir," Rachel said; "I saw him shoot through the bay window and then I ran away."

Whereupon, she repeated the action at the conclusion of her statement, and hurried away. "Humph!" said Fleming Stone.

CHAPTER 15: THE AWFUL TRUTH

"Well, Fibs," said Stone, as the two sat alone in conclave, "what about Rachel's story?"

"You know, F. Stone, how I hate to doubt a lady's word, but—not to put too fine a point upon it, the fair Rachel lied."

"You think so, too, eh? And just why?"

"Under orders. She was coached in her part. Told exactly what to say—"

"By whom?"

"Oh, you know as well as I do. You're just leading me on! Well, he coached her, all right, and she got scared before the performance came off and that's why she ran away."

"Yes, I agree to all that. Keefe, of course, being the coach."

"Yessir. He doing it, to save the Wheelers. You see, he's so desperately in love with Miss Maida, that it sort of blinds his judgment and cleverness,"

"Just how?"

"Well, you know his is love at first sight—practically."

"Look here, Terence, you know a great deal about love."

"Yessir, it—it comes natural to me. I'm a born lover, I am."

"Had much experience?"

"Not yet. But my day's coming. Well, never mind me—to get back to Friend Keefe. Here's the way it is. Miss Wheeler is sort of engaged to Mr. Allen, and yet the matter isn't quite settled, either. I get that from the servants—mean to gossip, but all's fair in love and sleuthing. Now, Mr. Keefe comes along, sees the lovely Maida, and, zip! his heart is cracked! All might yet be

well, but for the wily Genevieve. She has her cap set for
Keefe, and he knows it, and was satisfied it should be so,
till he saw Miss Wheeler. Now, the fat's in the fire, and
no pitch hot."

"You do pick up a lot of general information."

"It's necess'ry, sir." The red-head nodded
emphatically. "These sidelights often point the way to the
great and shinin' truth! For, don't you see, Mr. Keefe,
being so gone on Miss Maida, naturally doesn't want her
or her people suspected of this crime—even if one of them
is guilty. So he fixes up a cock-and-bull story about a
bugler man—on the south veranda. This man, he argues,
did the shooting. He gets Rachel—he must have some
hold on her, bribery wouldn't be enough—and he fair
crams the bugler yarn down her throat, and orders her to
recite it as Gospel truth."

"Then she gets scared and runs away."

"Exactly. You see it that way, don't you, Mr. Stone?"

The earnest little face looked up to the master.
Terence McGuire was developing a wonderful gift for
psychological detective work, and sometimes he let his
imagination run away with him. In such cases Stone
tripped him up and turned him back to the right track.
Both had an inkling that the day might eventually come
when Stone would retire and McGuire would reign in his
stead. But this was, as yet, merely a dream, and at
present they worked together in unison and harmony.

"Yes, Fibsy—at least, I see it may have been that way.
But it's a big order to put on—to Mr. Keefe."

"I know, but he's a big man. I mean a man of big
notions and projects. Anybody can see that. Now, he's
awful anxious Miss Wheeler and Mr. Wheeler shall be
cleared of all s'picion—even if he thinks one of 'em is
guilty. He doesn't consider Mrs. Wheeler—I guess nobody
does now."

"Probably not. Goon."

"Well, so Keefie, he thinks if he can get this bugler
person guaranteed, by a reliable and responsible

witness—which, of course, Rachel would seem to be—then, Mr. Keefe thinks, he's got the Wheelers cleared. Now, Rachel, getting cold feet about it all, goes back on Keefe—oh, I could see it in his face!"

"Yes, he looked decidedly annoyed at Rachel's failure of a convincing performance."

"He did so! Now, Mr. Stone, even if he bolsters up Rachel's story or gets her to tell it more convincingly—we know, you and I, that it isn't true. There wasn't any man on the south veranda."

"Sure, Terence?"

"Yessir, I'm pretty sure. For, what became of him? Where did he vanish to? Who was he? There never was any bugler—I mean as a murderer. The piper who piped some nights previous had nothing to do with the case!"

"Sure, Terence?"

"Oh, come now, Mr. Stone—I was sure, till you say that at me, so dubious like—and then I'm not..."

"Well, go on with your theory, and let's see where you come out. You may be on the right track, after all. I'm not sure of many points myself yet."

"All right. To my mind, it comes back to a toss-up between Miss Maida and her father, with the odds in favor of the old gentleman. Agree?"

"I might, if I understood your English. The odds in favor of Mr. Wheeler indicating his guilt or innocence?"

"His guilt, I meant, F. Stone. I can't think that sweet young lady would do it, and this isn't because she is a sweet young lady, but because it isn't hardly plausible that she's put the thing over, even though she was willing enough to do so."

"It seems so to me, too, but we can't bank on that. Maida Wheeler is a very impulsive girl, very vigorous and athletic, and very devoted to her father. She worships him, and she has been known to say she would willingly kill old Mr. Appleby. These things must be remembered, Fibsy."

"That's so. But I've noticed that when folks threaten to kill people they most generally don't do it."

"I've also noticed that. But, striking out Maida's name, leaves us only Mr. Wheeler."

"Well, ain't he the one? Ain't he the downtrodden, oppressed victim, who, at last, has opportunity, and who is goaded to the point of desperation by the arguments of his enemy?"

"You grow oratorical! But, I admit, you have an argument."

"'Course I have. Now, say we've got to choose between Miss Wheeler and Mr. Wheeler, how do we go about it?"

"How?"

"Why, we find out how Mr. Appleby was sitting, how Mr. Wheeler was facing at the moment, and also Miss Maida's position. Then, we find out the direction from which the bullet entered the body, and then we can tell who fired the shot."

"I've done all that, Fibs," Stone returned, with no note of superiority in his voice. "I found out all those things, and the result proves that the bullet entered Mr. Appleby's body from the direction of Miss Maida, in the bay window, and directly opposite from what would have been its direction if fired by Mr. Wheeler, from where he stood, when seen directly after the shot."

Fibsy looked dejected. He made no response to this disclosure for a moment, then he said:

"All right, F. Stone. In that case I'm going over to Mr. Keefe's side, and I'm going to hunt up the bugler."

"A fictitious person?"

"Maybe he ain't so fictitious after all," and the redhead shook doggedly.

A tap at the door of Stone's sitting-room was followed by a "May I come in?" and the entrance of Daniel Wheeler.

"The time has come, Mr. Wheeler," Stone began a little abruptly, "to put all our cards on the table. I've investigated things pretty thoroughly, and, though I'm not all through with my quest, I feel as if I must know the truth as to what you know about the murder."

"I have confessed," Wheeler began, but Stone stopped him.

"That won't do," he said, very seriously. "I've proved positively that from where you stood, you could not have fired the shot. It came from the opposite direction. Now it's useless for you to keep up that pretence of being the criminal, which, I've no doubt, you're doing to shield your daughter. Confide in me, Mr. Wheeler, it will not harm the case."

"God help me, I must confide in somebody," cried the desperate man. "She did do it! I saw Maida fire the shot! Oh, can you save her? I wouldn't tell you this, but I think—I hope you can help better if you know. You'd find it out anyway—"

"Of course I should. Now, let us be strictly truthful. You saw Miss Maida fire the pistol?"

"Yes; I was sitting almost beside Appleby; he was nearer Maida than I was, and she sat in the bay window, reading. She sits there much of the time, and I'm so accustomed to her presence that I don't even think about it. We were talking pretty angrily, Appleby and I, really renewing the old feud, and adding fuel to its flame with every word. I suppose Maida, listening, grew more and more indignant at his injustice and cruelty to me—those terms are not too strong!—and she being of an impulsive nature, even revengeful when her love for me is touched, and I suppose she, somehow, possessed herself of my pistol and fired it."

"You were not looking at her before the shot?"

"Oh, no; the shot rang out, Appleby fell forward, and even as I rose to go to his aid, I instinctively turned toward the direction from which the sound of the shot had come. There I saw Maida, standing white-faced and frightened, but with a look of satisfied revenge on her dear face. I felt no resentment at her act, then—indeed, I was incapable of coherent thought of any sort. I stepped!

to Appleby's side, and I saw at once that he was dead—
had died instantly. I cannot tell you just what happened
next. It seemed ages before anybody came, and then,
suddenly the room was full of people. Allen and Keefe
came, running—the servants gathered about, my wife
appeared, and Maida was there. I had a strange
undercurrent of thought that kept hammering at my
brain to the effect that I must convince everybody that I
did it, to save my girl. I was clear-headed to the extent of
planning my words in an effort to carry conviction of my
guilt, but that effort so absorbed my attention that I gave
no heed to what happened otherwise."

"Thank you, Mr. Wheeler, for your kindness. I assure
you you will not regret it."

"You're going to save her? You can save my little girl?
Oh, Mr. Stone, I beg of you—"

The agonized father broke down completely, and
Stone said, kindly:

"Keep up a good heart, Mr. Wheeler. That will help
your daughter more than anything else you can do. I
assumed that if one of you were guilty the other was
shielding the criminal, but your story has straightened
out the tangle considerably."

"Lemme ask something, please," broke in Fibsy. "Say,
Mr. Wheeler, did you see the pistol in Miss MaMa's
hands?"

"I can't say I did or didn't," Wheeler replied, listlessly.
"I looked only at her face. I know my daughter's mind so
well, that I at once recognized her expression of horror
mingled with relief. She had really desired the death of
her father's enemy, and she was glad it had been
·accomplished! It's a terrible thing to say of one's own
child, but I've made up my mind to be honest with you,
Mr. Stone, in the hope of your help. I should have
persisted in my own story of guilt, had I not perceived it
was futile in the face of your clear-sighted logic and
knowledge of the exact circumstances."

"You did wisely. But say nothing to any one else, for the present. Do not even talk to Miss Maida about it, until I have time to plan our next step. It is still a difficult and a very delicate case. A single false move may queer the whole game."

"You think, then, you can save Maida—oh, do give a tortured father a gleam of hope!"

"I shall do my best. You know they rarely, if ever, convict a woman—and, too, Miss Wheeler had great provocation. Then—what about self-defence?"

"Appleby threatened neither of us," Wheeler said. "That can't be used."

"Well, we'll do everything we can, you may depend on that," Stone assured him. And Wheeler went away, relieved at the new turn things had taken, though also newly concerned for Maida's safety.

"Nice old chap," said Fibsy to Stone. "He stuck to his faked yarn as long as the sticking was good, and then he caved in."

"Open and shut case, Terence?"

"Open—but not yet shut, F. Stone. Now, where do we go from here?"

"You go where you like, boy. Leave me to grub at this alone."

Without another word Fibsy left the room. He well knew when Stone spoke in that serious tone that great thoughts were forming in that fertile brain and sooner or later he would know of them. But at present his company was not desired.

The boy drifted out on the terraced lawn and wandered about among the gardens. He, too, thought, but he could see no light ahead.

"S'long as the old man saw her," he observed to himself, "there's no more to be said. He never'd say he saw her shoot, if he hadn't seen her. He's at the end of his rope, and even if they acquit the lady I don't want to see her dragged through a trial. But where's any way of escape? What can turn up to contradict a straight story like that? Who else can testify except the eye-witness who has just spoken? I wonder if he realized himself how conclusive his statement was? But he trusted in F. Stone to get Maida off, somehow. Queer, how most folks think a detective is a magician, and can do the impossible trick!"

In a brown study he walked slowly along the garden paths, and was seen by Keefe and Maida, who sat under the big sycamore tree.

"Crazy idea, Stone bringing that kid," Keefe said, with a laugh.

"Yes, but he's a very bright boy," Maida returned. "I've been surprised at his wise observations."

"Poppycock! He gets off his speeches with that funny mixture of newsboy slang and detective jargon, and you think they're cleverer than they are."

"Perhaps," agreed Maida, not greatly interested. "But what a strange story Rachel told. Do you believe it, Mr. Keefe?"

"Yes, I do. The girl was frightened, I think; first, at the information she tried to divulge, and second, by finding herself in the limelight. She seems to be shy, and I daresay the sudden publicity shook her nerves. But why shouldn't her story be true? Why should she invent all that?"

"I don't know, I'm sure. But it didn't sound like Rachel—the whole thing, I mean. She seemed acting a part."

"Nonsense! You imagine that. But never mind her, I've something to tell you. I know—Maida, mind you, I know what Mr. Appleby meant by the speech which I took to be 'Mr. Keefe and the airship.'"

Maida's face went white.

"Oh, no!" she cried, involuntarily. "Oh, no!"

"Yes," Keefe went on, "and I know now he said heirship. Not strange I misunderstood, for the words are of the same sound—and, then I had no reason to think of myself in connection with an heirship!"

"And—and have you now?"

"Yes, I have. I've been over Mr. Appleby's papers—as I had a right to do. You know I was his confidential secretary, and he kept no secrets from me—except those he wanted to keep!"

"Go on," said Maida, calm now, and her eyes glistening with an expression of despair.

"Need I go on? You know the truth. You know that I am the rightful heir of this whole place. Sycamore Ridge is mine, and not your mother's."

"Yes." The word was scarce audible. Poor Maida felt as if the last blow had fallen. She had seared her conscience, defied her sense of honor, crucified her very soul to keep this dreadful secret from her parents for their own sake, and now all her efforts were of no avail!

Curtis Keefe knew that the great estate was legally his, and now her dear parents would be turned out, homeless, penniless and broken down by sorrow and grief.

Even though he might allow them to stay there, they wouldn't, she knew, consent to any such arrangement.

She lifted a blanched, strained face to his, as she said: "What—what are you going to do?"

"Just what you say," Keefe replied, drawing closer to her side. "It's all up to you, Maida dear. Don't look offended; surely you know I love you—surely you know my one great desire is to make you my wife. Give your consent; say you will be mine, and rest assured, dearest, there will be no trouble about the 'heirship.' If you will marry me, I will promise never to divulge the secret so long as either of your parents live. They may keep this place, and, besides that, darling, I will guarantee to get your father a full pardon. I—well, I'm not speaking of it yet—but I'll tell you that there is a possibility of my running for governor myself, since young Sam is voluntarily out of it. But, in any case, I have influence enough in certain quarters—influence increased by knowledge that I have gleaned here and there among the late Mr. Appleby's papers—to secure a full and free pardon for your father. Now, Maida, girl, even if you don't love me very much yet, can't you say yes, in view of what I offer you?"

"How can you torture me so? Surely you know that I am engaged to Mr. Allen."

"I didn't know it was a positive engagement—but, anyway," his voice grew hard, "it seems to me that any one so solicitous for her parents' welfare and happiness as you have shown yourself, will not hesitate at a step which means so much more than others you have taken."

"Oh, I don't know what to do—what to say—let me think."

"Yes, dear, think all you like. Take it quietly now. Remember that a decision in my favor means also a calm, peaceful and happy life insured to your parents. Refusal means a broken, shattered life, a precarious existence, and never a happy day for them again. Can you hesitate? I'm not so very unpresentable as a husband. You may not love me now, but you will! I'll be so good to you that you can't help it. Nor do I mean to win your heart only by what I shall do for you. For, Maida dearest, love begets love, and you will find yourself slowly perhaps, but surely, giving me your heart. And we will be so happy! Is it yes, my darling?"

The girl stared at him, her big brown eyes full of agony.

"You forget something," she said, slowly. "I am a murderess!"

"Hush! Don't say that awful word! You are not—and even if you were, I'll prove you are not! Listen, Maida, if you'll promise to marry me, I'll find the real murderer— not you or your father, but the real murderer. I'll get a signed confession—I'll acquit you and your family of any implication in the deed, and I'll produce the criminal himself. Now, will you say yes?"

"You can't do all that," she said, speaking in an awestruck whisper, as if he had proposed to perform a miracle.

"I can—I swear it!"

"Then, if you can do that, you ought to do it, anyway! In the interests of right and justice, in common honesty and decency, you ought to tell what you know!"

"Maida, I am a man and I am in love with you. That explains much. I will do all I have promised, to gain you as my bride—but not otherwise. As to right and justice—you've confessed the crime, haven't you?"

"Yes."

"Do you confess it to me, now? Do you say to me that you killed Samuel Appleby?"

There was but a moment's pause, and then Maida said, in a low tone: "Yes—I confess it to you, Mr. Keefe."

"Then, do you see what I mean when I say I will produce the murderer? Do you see that I mean to save you from the consequences of your own rash act—and prove you, to the world at large, innocent?"

Keefe looked straight into Maida's eyes, and her own fell in confusion.

"Can you do it?" she asked, tremulously.

"When I say I will do a thing, I've already proved to my own satisfaction that I can do it. But, I'll do it only at my own price. The price being you—you dear, delicious thing! Oh, Maida, you've no idea what it means to be loved as I love you! I'll make you happy, my darling! I'll make you forget all this horrible episode; I'll give you a fairyland life. You shall be happier than you ever dreamed of."

"But—Jeffrey—oh, I can't."

"Then—Miss Wheeler, you must take the consequences—all the consequences. Can you do that?"

"No," Maida said, after an interval of silence, "I can't. I am forced to accept your offer, Mr. Keefe—"

"You may not accept it with that address."

"Curtis, then. Curtis, I say, yes."

Chapter 16: Maida's Decision

"Maida, it cannot be. I shall never let you marry Mr. Keefe when I know how you love Jeffrey." Sara Wheeler spoke quietly, but her agonized face and tear-filled eyes told of her deep distress. Though not demonstrative, she loved her daughter, her only child, with an affection that was almost idolatry, and she had been glad of the idea of Maida's marriage to Jeffrey, for she knew of his sterling worth, and she knew the depth and sincerity of their attachment.

"Don't say you won't let me, mother," Maida spoke in a dull, sad tone—a tone of calm despair. "It must be so. I'm not saying I love him—I'm not saying much about it all—but I tell you solemnly—it must be. And you must not raise a single word of objection—if you do, you will only make my hard lot harder."

"But, dear, you must explain. I am your mother—I've always had your confidence, and I ought to be told why you are doing this thing."

"That's just the trouble, mother. I can't tell you. And because of the confidence that has always been between us, you must trust me and believe that I am doing right—and doing the only possible thing. Oh, it is all hard enough, without having to argue about it. Why, my will power may give out! My soul strength may break down! Mother! don't—don't combat me! Don't tempt me aside from the only straight line of duty and of right!"

"Child, you are not doing right! You cannot have a duty of which I know nothing! Of which your father knows nothing! Maida, my little girl, what is this thing that has warped your sense of right and wrong? Has Curtis Keefe won your heart away from Jeffrey—"

"No—oh, no! Never that! But it would be a wrong to Jeffrey for me to marry him—it would be a wrong to—to all of us! By marrying Mr. Keefe I can make everything right—and—" she suddenly assumed an air of cold, stern determination. "Mother, my mind is made up. You cannot change it, nor can you help me by trying. You only make it harder for me, and I beg of you to stop. And then—you know, mother—I killed Mr. Appleby—"

"Hush, Maida, you never did! I know you didn't!"

"But it was either I or father! You don't believe he did, do you?"

"God help me! I don't know what to believe! But I tried to say I did it—only I couldn't carry it out—nor can you, dear."

"Nor can father, then. Oh, mother, I did do that shooting! I did! I did!"

"Every assertion like that makes me more certain you didn't," and Mrs. Wheeler fondly caressed the head that lay on her breast. Maida was not hysterical, but so deeply troubled that she was nervously unstrung and now gave way to torrents of tears, and then ceased crying and bravely announced her plans.

"Please, mother darling, don't talk about that. Suppose I tell you that even that matter will be all set right if I marry Curtis Keefe—and by no other means. Even Mr. Stone can't find any other suspect than us three Wheelers. He doesn't at all believe in the 'bugler.' Nobody does."

"I do."

"Only as a last chance to free father and me. Mother it's an awful situation. Worse, far worse than you know anything about. Won't you trust me to do what I know to be right—and when I tell you I must marry Mr. Keefe, won't you believe me?And not only believe me but help me. Help me in every way you can—for God knows I need help."

"What can I do, darling," asked Sara Wheeler, awed by the look of utter hopelessness on Maida's face,

"Stand by me, mother. Urge father not to oppose this marriage. Help me to tell Jeffrey—you tell him, can't you, mother? I can't—oh, I can't!"

Again Sara Wheeler broke out into protestations against this sacrifice of her loved daughter, and again Maida had to reaffirm her decision, until, both worn out, they separated, Sara promising to do just as Maida wished in all things.

And in fulfillment of this promise, Sara told young Allen.

As she expected, he was stunned by the news, but where she had supposed he would show anger or rage, he showed only a deep sympathy for Maida.

"Poor little girl," he said, the quick tears springing to his eyes; "what dreadful thing can that man have held over her to force her to this? And what is the best way for me to go about remedying the situation? You know, Mrs. Wheeler, Maida wouldn't talk like that unless she had arrived at a very desperate crisis—"

"If she killed Mr. Appleby—"

"She never did! No power on earth can make me believe that! Why, when Maida's own confession doesn't convince me, what else could? No; there's some deep mystery behind that murder. I mean something far deeper and more mysterious than any of us yet realize. I think Mr. Stone is on track of the solution, but he cannot have made much progress—or, if he has, he hasn't told of it yet. But, I'm not a detective—nor is any needed when Mr. Stone is on the case, but I am out to protect and clear my Maida—my darling. Poor child, how she is suffering! Where is she?"

"Don't go to her, Jeff. At least, not just now. She begged that you wouldn't—"

"But I must—I've got to!"

"No; for her sake—Jeffrey dear, for our Maida's sake, leave her alone for the present. She is so worried and anxious, so wrought up to the very verge of collapse, that if you try to talk to her she will go all to pieces."

"But that's all wrong. I ought to soothe her, to comfort her—not make her more troubled!"

"You ought to, I know, but you wouldn't. Oh, it isn't your fault—it isn't that you don't love her enough—not that she doesn't love you enough—in fact, that's just the trouble. Try to see it, Jeff. Maida is in the clutch of circumstances. I don't know the facts, you don't; but it is true that the kindest thing we can do for her just now is to leave her alone. She will do right—"

"As she sees it, yes! But she sees wrong, I know she does! The child has always been over conscientious—and I'm positive that whatever she is up to, it's something to save her father!"

"Oh, Jeff—then you believe he is—"

"Why, Mrs. Wheeler, don't you know whether your husband killed Mr. Appleby or not?"

"I don't know! Heaven help me—how can I know? The two of them, shielding each other—"

"Wait a minute, if they are shielding each other—they're both innocent!"

"But it isn't that way. Mr. Wheeler said to me, at first: "Of course, either Maida or I did it. We both know which one did it, but if we don't tell, no one else can know.""

"I see that point; but I should think, knowing both so closely as you do, you could discern the truth—and—" he gazed at her steadily—"you have."

"Yes—I have. Of course, as you say, in such intimacy as we three are, it would be impossible for me not to know."

"And—it was Maida?"

"Yes, Jeffrey."

"How are you certain?"

"Her father saw her."

"Saw her shoot?"

"Yes."

"Then, I'm glad you told me. I'm going to marry her at once, and have all rights of her protection through the trial—if it comes to that. Nothing else could have convinced me of her act! Poor, dear little Maida. I've known her capability for sudden, impulsive action but—oh, well, if Mr. Wheeler saw her—that's all there is to be said. Now, dear Mrs. Wheeler, you must let me go to my Maida!"

"But, Jeffrey, I only told you that to persuade you to let her alone. Let her have her own way. She says that to marry Curtis Keefe will save her from prosecution—even from suspicion. She says he can free her from all implication in the matter."

"By a fraud?"

"I don't know—"

"I won't have it! If Maida did that shooting she had ample excuse—motive, rather. Not a man on a jury would convict her. And I'd rather she'd stand trial and—"

"Oh, no, Jeffrey, don't talk like that! I'd consent to anything to save that girl from a trial—oh, you can't mean you want her tried!"

"Rather than to see her married to any man but me, I'd—"

"Wait, Jeff. We mustn't be selfish. I'm her mother, and much as I'd hate to see her marry Keefe, I'd far prefer it—for her sake, than—"

"No! a thousand times, no! Why, I won't give her up! Keefe is a fine man—I've nothing against him—but she's my Maida—my own little sweetheart—"

"And for that reason—for your own sake—you're going to claim her?"

"It isn't only for my own sake "—Jeff spoke more humbly; "but I know—I know how she loves me. To let her marry another would be to do her a grievous wrong—"

"Not if she wants to—look there!"

Mrs. Wheeler pointed from the window, and they saw Maida walking across the lawn in deep and earnest conversation with Curtis Keefe. He was tall and handsome and the deferential air and courteous attitude all spoke in his favor. Maida was apparently listening with interest to his talk, and they went on slowly toward the old sycamore and sat down on the bench beneath it.

"Our trysting—place!" Jeffrey murmured, his eyes fastened on the pair.

It did not require over-close observation to see that Maida was listening willingly to Keefe. Nor was there room for doubt that he was saying something that pleased her. She was brighter and more cheerful than she had been for days.

"You see," said Sara Wheeler, sadly. "And he is a worth-while man. Mr. Appleby thought very highly of him."

"I don't!" said Allen, briefly, and unable to stand any more, he left the room.

He went straight to the two who were sitting under the big tree, and spoke directly:

"What does this mean, Maida? Your mother tells me you—"

"Let me answer," spoke up Keefe, gaily; "it means that Miss Wheeler has promised to marry me. And we ask your congratulations."

"Are you not aware," Jeff's face was white but his voice was controlled and steady, "that Miss Wheeler is my fiancee?"

"Hardly that," demurred Keefe. "I believe there was what is called an understanding, but I'm assured it has never been announced. However, the lady will speak for herself."

"Go away, Jeff," Maida pleaded; "please, go away."

"Not until you tell me yourself, Maida, what you are doing. Why does Mr. Keefe say these things?"

"It is true." Maida's face was as white as Allen's. "I am going to marry Mr. Keefe. If you considered me bound to you, I hereby break it off. Please go away!" the last words were wrung from her in a choked, agonized voice, as if she were at the end of her composure.

"I'm going," Allen said, and went off in a daze.

He was convinced of one thing only. That Maida was in the power of something or some person—some combination of circumstances that forced her to this. He had no doubt she meant what she said; had no doubt she would really marry Keefe—but he couldn't think she had ceased to love him—her own Jeffrey! If he thought that, he was ready to die!

He walked along half blindly, thinking round in circles, always coming back to the possibility—now practically a certainty—of Maida being the murderer, and wondering how Keefe meant to save her from the clutches of the law. He was perturbed—almost dazed, and as he went along unseeingly, Genevieve Lane met him, turned and walked by his side.

"What's Curtis Keefe doing with your girl?" she asked, for the rolling lawn was so free of trees, the pair beneath the sycamore could be plainly seen.

"I don't know!" said Allen, honestly enough, as he looked in the good-humored face of the stenographer.

"I don't want him making love to her," Miss Lane went on, pouting a little, "first, because she's altogether too much of a belle anyway; and second—because "

She paused, almost scared at the desperate gaze Allen gave her.

"I hope you mean because you look upon him as your property," he said, but without smiling.

"Now, just why do you hope that?"

"Because in that case, surely you can get him back—"

"Oh, what an aspersion on Miss Wheeler's fascinations!"

"Hush; I'm in no mood for chaffing. Are you and Keefe special friends?"

Genevieve looked at him a moment, and then said, very frankly: "If we're not, it isn't my fault. And to tell you the bald truth, we would have been, had not Miss Wheeler come between us."

"Are you sure of that?"

"How rude you are! But, yes—I'm practically sure. Nobody can be sure till they're certain, you know."

"Don't try to joke with me. Look here, Miss Lane, suppose you and I try to work together for our respective ends."

"Meaning just what, Mr. Allen?"

"Meaning that we try to separate Keefe and Maida— not just at this moment—but seriously and permanently. You, because you want him, and I, because I want her. Isn't it logical?"

"Yes; but if I could get him back, don't you suppose I would?"

"You don't get the idea. You're to work for me, and I for you."

"Oh—I try to make Maida give him up—and you—"

"Yes; but we must have some pretty strong arguments. Now, have you any idea why Maida has—"

"Has picked him up with the tongs? I have a very decided idea! In fact, I know."

"You do! Is it a secret?"

"It is. Such a big secret, that if it leaked out, the whole universe, so far as it affects the Wheeler family, would be turned topsy-turvy!"

"Connected with the—the death of Mr. Appleby?"

"Not with the murder—if that's what you mean. But it was because of the death of Mr. Appleby that the secret came to light."

"Can you tell me?"

"I can—but do I want to?"

"What would make you want to?"

"Why—only if you could do what you sort of suggested—make Mr. Keefe resume his attentions to poor little Genevieve and leave the lovely Maida to you."

"But how can I do that?"

"Dunno, I'm sure! Do you want me to tell you the secret, and then try to get my own reward by my own efforts?"

"Oh, I don't know what I want! I'm nearly distracted. But—" he pulled himself together—"I'm on the job! And I'm going to accomplish something—a lot! Now, I'm not going to dicker with you. Size it up for yourself. Don't you believe that if you told me that secret—confidentially— except as it can be used in the furtherance of right and happiness for all concerned—don't you believe that I might use it in a way that would incidentally result in a better adjustment of the present Keefe-Wheeler combination?" He nodded toward the two under the sycamore.

"Maybe," Genevieve said, slowly and thoughtfully, "I thought of telling Mr. Stone—but—"

"Tell me first, and let me advise you."

"I will; I have confidence in you, Mr. Allen, and, too, it may be a good thing to keep the secret in the family. The truth is, then, that Mrs. Wheeler is not legally the heir to this estate."

"She is, if she lives in Massachusetts, and the house is so built—"

"Oh, fiddlesticks! I don't mean that part of it. The estate is left with the proviso that the inheritor shall live in Massachusetts—but, what I mean is, that it isn't left to Mrs. Wheeler at all. She thought it was, of course—but there is another heir."

"Is there? I've often heard them speak of such a possibility but they never could find a trace of one,"

"I know it, and they're so honest that if they knew of one they'd put up no fight. I mean if they knew there is a real heir, and that Sara Wheeler is not the right inheritor."

"Who is?"

"Curtis Keefe!"

"Oh, no! Miss Lane, are you sure?"

"I am. I discovered it from Mr. Appleby's private papers, since his death."

"Does Keefe know it?"

"Of course; but he doesn't know I know it. Now, see here, Mr. Allen, get this. Mr. Appleby knew it when he came down here. He—this is only my own theory, but I'll bet it's the right one—he had discovered it lately; Keefe didn't know it. My theory is, that he came down here to hold that knowledge as a dub over the head of Mr. Wheeler to force him to do his, Appleby's, bidding in the campaign matters. Well, then—he was killed to prevent the information going any farther."

"Killed by whom?"

Genevieve shrugged her shoulders. "I can't say. Any one of the three Wheelers might have done it for that reason."

"No; you're wrong. Neither Mr. nor Mrs. Wheeler would have. They'd give up the place at once."

"Your mental reservation speaks for itself! That leaves Maida! Suppose she knew it and the rest didn't. Suppose, in order to keep the knowledge from her parents—"

"Don't go on!" he begged. "I see it—maybe it was so. But—what next?"

"Next—alas, Curt Keefe has fallen a victim to Maida's smiles. That's what's making more trouble than anything else. I'm positive he is arguing that if she will marry him he will keep quiet about his being the heir. Then, her parents can live here in peace for the rest of their lives."

"I begin to see."

"I knew you would. Now, knowing this, and being bound to secrecy concerning it, except, as you agreed, if it can serve our ends, where do we go from here?"

Allen looked at her steadily. "Do you expect, Miss Lane, that I will consent to keep this secret from the Wheelers?"

"You'll have to," she returned, simply. "Maida knows it, therefore it's her secret now. If she doesn't want her parents told—you can't presume to tell them!"

Allen looked blank. "And you mean, she'd marry Keefe, to keep the secret from her parents?"

"Exactly that; and there'd be no harm in keeping the secret that way, for if Curt Keefe were her husband, it wouldn't matter whether he was the rightful heir or not, if he didn't choose to exercise or even make known his rights."

"I see. And—as to the—"

"The murder?" Genevieve helped him. "Well, I don't know. If Maida did it—and I can't see any way out of that conclusion, Curt will do whatever he can to get her off easily. Perhaps he can divert suspicion elsewhere—you know he made up that bugler man, and has stuck to him—maybe he can get a persons unknown verdict—or maybe, with money and influence, he can hush the whole thing up—and, anyway—Maida would never be convicted. Why, possibly, the threat of Mr. Appleby—if he did threaten—could be called blackmail. Anyhow, if there's a loophole, Curtis Keefe will find it! He's as smart as they make 'em. Now, you know the probabilities— almost the inevitabilities, I might say, what are we going to do about it?"

"Something pretty desperate, I can tell you!"

"Fine talk, but what's the first step?"

"Do you want to know what I think?"

"I sure do."

"Then, I say, let's take the whole story to Fleming Stone—and at once."

CHAPTER 17: MAIDA AND HER FATHER

Genevieve hesitated. Although she had thought of doing this herself, yet she was not quite sure she wanted to.

But Allen insisted.

"Come with me or not, as you choose," he said; "but I'm going to tell Stone. A secret like that must be divulged—in the interests of law and justice and—"

"Justice to whom?" asked Genevieve.

"Why, to all concerned." Allen stopped to think. "To—to Keefe, for one," he concluded, a little lamely.

"Yes, and to yourself for two!" Genevieve exclaimed. "You want the secret to come out so Maida won't marry Curt to keep it quiet! Own up, now."

Allen couldn't deny this, but back of it was his instinctive desire for justice all round, and he doggedly stuck to his determination of laying the matter before Fleming Stone.

Genevieve accompanied him, and together they sought Stone in his sitting-room.

Fibsy was there and the two were in deep consultation.

"Come in," Stone said, as his visitors appeared. "You have something to tell me, I gather from your eager faces."

"We have," Allen returned, and he began to tell his story.

"Let me tell it," Miss Lane interrupted him, impatiently. "You see, Mr. Stone, Mr. Allen is in love with Miss Wheeler, and he can't help coloring things in her favor."

"And you're in love with Mr. Keefe," Stone said, but without a smile, "and you can't help coloring things in his favor."

The girl bridled a little, but was in no way embarrassed at the assertion.

"Take your choice, then," she said, flippantly. "Who do you want to tell you the secret we're ready to give away?"

"Both," Fibsy spoke up. "I'll bet it's a worthwhile yarn, and we'll hear both sides—if you please. Ladies first; pipe up, Miss Lane."

"The actual secret can be quickly told," the girl said, speaking a little shortly. "The truth is, that Mrs. Wheeler is not the legal heir to this estate of Sycamore Ridge— but, Mr. Keefe is."

"Curtis Keefe!" Stone exclaimed, and Fibsy gave a sharp, explosive whistle.

"Yes," said Genevieve, well pleased at the sensation her words had produced.

Not that her hearers made any further demonstration of surprise. Stone fell into a brown study, and Fibsy got up and walked up and down the room, his hands in his pockets, and whistling softly under his breath,

"Well!" the boy said, finally, returning to his chair. "Well, F. Stone, things is changed since gran'ma died! Hey?"

"In many ways!" Stone assented. "You're sure of this, of course?" he asked Genevieve. "How do you know?"

"Well, I learned it from Mr. Appleby's papers—"

"Private papers?"

"Yes, of course. He didn't have 'em framed and hanging on his wall. You see, Mr. Keefe, being Mr. Appleby's confidential secretary, had access to all his papers after the old gentleman died."

"His son?"

"Of course, young Sam is the heir, and owns everything, but he kept Curt on, in the same position, and so, Curt—Mr. Keefe went over all the papers. As stenographer and general assistant, I couldn't very well help knowing the contents of the papers and so I learned the truth, that Mr. Keefe, who is of another branch of the family, is really the principal heir to the estate that is now in Mrs. Wheeler's possession. I can't give you all the actual details, but you can, of course, verify my statements."

"Of course," mused Stone. "And Mr. Keefe hasn't announced this himself—because—"

"That's it," Genevieve nodded assent to his meaning glance. "Because he wants to marry Maida, and if she'll marry him, he'll keep quiet about the heirship. Or, rather, in that case, it won't matter, as the elder Wheelers can live here if it's the property of their son-in-law. But, if not, then when Mr. Keefe walks in—the Wheeler family must walk out. And where would they go?"

"I can take care of them," declared Allen. "Maida is my promised wife; if she consents to marry Keefe, it will be under compulsion. For she knew this secret, and she dared not tell her people because it meant poverty and homelessness for them. You know, Mr. Wheeler is incapable of lucrative work, and Mrs. Wheeler, brought up to affluence and comfort, can't be expected to live in want. But I can take care of them—that is, I could—if they could only live in Boston. My business is there, and we could all live on my earnings if we could live together."

The boy—for young Allen seemed scarcely more than a boy—was really thinking aloud as he voiced these plans and suggestions. But he shook his head sadly as he realized that Daniel Wheeler couldn't go to Boston, and that a marriage between Keefe and Maida was the only way to preserve to them their present home.

"Some situation!" remarked Fibsy. "And the secret is no secret really, for if Miss Wheeler doesn't marry Mr. Keefe, he'll tell it at once. And if she does, the whole matter doesn't matter at all! But I think she will, for what else can she do?"

Jeffrey Allen looked angrily at the boy, but Fibsy's funny little face showed such a serious interest that it was impossible to chide him.

"I think she won't!" Allen said, "but I'm not sure just yet how I'm going to prevent it."

"You won't have to," said Stone; "Miss Wheeler will prevent it herself—or I miss my guess!" He looked kindly at the young man, but received only a half smile in return,

"If we all do our share in the matter, perhaps we can arrange things," Genevieve said, speaking very seriously. "I've something to say, for I am engaged to Curtis Keefe myself."

"Does he think you are?" Stone said, rather casually.

Miss Lane had the grace to blush, through her rouge, but she declared: "He doesn't want to," and added, "but he ought to. He has made love to me, and he once asked me to marry him. But since then he has said he didn't mean it. I don't suppose I've enough evidence for a breach of promise suit, but—oh, well," and she tossed her pretty head, "I've not the least doubt that if Miss Wheeler were out of the question—say, safely married to Mr. Allen, I'd have no trouble in whistling my Turtle back."

"I'll bet you wouldn't!" Fibsy looked at her admiringly. "If I were only a few years older—"

"Hush, Terence," said Fleming Stone, "don't talk nonsense."

Immediately Fibsy's face became serious and he turned has attention away from the fascinating Genevieve.

"But all this is aside the question of the murderer, Mr. Stone," said Allen. "How are you progressing with that investigation?"

"Better than I've disclosed as yet," Stone returned, speaking slowly; "recent developments have been helpful, and I hope to be ready soon to give a report."

"You expect Mr. Appleby down?"

"Yes; to-night or to-morrow. By that time I hope to be ready to make an arrest."

"Maida!" cried Jeffrey, the word seeming wrung from him against his will.

"Forgive me, if I do not reply," said Stone, with an earnest glance at the questioner. "But I'd like to talk to Miss Wheeler. Will you go for her, Mr. Allen?"

"I'd—I'd rather not—you see—"

"Yes, I see," said Stone, kindly. "You go, Fibs."

"I'll go," offered Genevieve, with the result that she and McGuire flew out of the room at the same time.

"All right, Beauteous One, we'll both go," Fibsy said, as they went along the hall side by side. "Where is the lady?"

"Donno; but we'll find her. I say, Terence, come down on the veranda just a minute, first."

Leading him to a far corner, where there was no danger of eavesdroppers, Genevieve made another attempt to gain an ally for her own cause.

"I say," she began, "you have a lot of influence with your Mr. Stone, don't you?"

"Oh, heaps!" and Fibsy's sweeping gesture indicated a wide expanse of imagination, at least.

"No fooling; I know you have. Now, you use that influence for me and I'll do something for you."

"What'll you do?"

"I don't know; nothing particular. But, I mean if, at any time I can help you in any way—I've influence, too, with big men in the financial and business world. I haven't always worked for the Applebys, and wherever I've been I've made friends that I can count on."

"Oh, you mean a tip on the stock market or something of that sort?"

"Yes, or a position in a big, worth-while office. You're not always going to be a detective's apprentice, are you?"

"You bet I am! Watcha talking about? Me leave F. Stone! Not on your fleeting existence! But, never mind that part of the argument, I'll remember your offer, and

some day, when I have a million dollars to invest, I'll ask
your advice where to lose it. But, now, you tell me what
you want."

"Only for you to hint to Mr. Stone that he'd better
advise Miss Wheeler not to marry Mr. Keefe."

"So's you can have him."

"Never mind that. There are other reasons—truly
there are."

"Well, then, my orders are to advise F. Stone to advise
M. Wheeler not to wed one C. Keefe."

"That's just it. But don't say it right out to him. Use
tact, which I know you have—though nobody'd guess it to
look at you—and sort of argue around, so he'll see it's
wiser for her not to marry him—"

"Why?"

Miss Lane stamped her foot impatiently. "I'm not
saying why. That's enough for me to know. You'll get
along better not knowing."

"Does he know she's the—the—"

"I don't wonder you can't say it! I can't, either. Yes, he
knows she's—it—but he's so crazy about her, he doesn't
care. What is there in that girl that gets all the men!"

"It's her sweetness," said Fibsy, with a positive nod of
his head, as if he were simply stating an axiom. "Yep,
Keefe is clean gone daffy over her. I don't blame him—
though, of course my taste runs more to—"

"Don't you dare!" cried Genevieve, coquettishly.

"To the rouged type," Fibsy went on, placidly. "To my
mind a complexion dabbed on is far more attractive than
nature's tints."

Miss Lane burst into laughter and, far from offended,
she said:

"You're a darling boy, and I'll never forget you—even
in my will; now, to come back to our dear old brass tacks.
Will you tip a gentle hint to the great Stone?"

"Oh, lord, yes—I'll tip him a dozen—tactfully, too.
Don't worry as to my discretion. But I don't mind telling

you I might as well tip the Washington monument. You see, F. S. has made up his mind,"

"As to the murderer?"

"Yep."

"Who is it?"

"Haven't an idea—and if I had, I'd say I hadn't. You see, I'm his trusty."

"Oh, well, in any case, you can put in a word against Mr. Keefe, can't you?"

But Genevieve had lost interest in her project. She realized if Mr. Stone had accomplished his purpose and had solved the murder mystery he would be apt to take small interest in the love affairs of herself or Maida Wheeler, either.

"He won't think much of his cherished trusty, if you don't do the errand he sent you on," she said, rather crossly.

Fibsy gave her a reproachful glance, "This, from you!" he said, dramatically. "Farewell, fair but false! I go to seek a fairer maiden, and I know where to find her!"

He went flying across the lawn, for he had caught a glimpse of Maida in the garden.

"Miss Wheeler," he said, as he reached her, "will you please come now to see Mr. Stone? He wants you."

"Certainly," she replied, and turning, followed him.

Genevieve joined them, and the three went to Stone's rooms.

"Miss Wheeler," the detective said, without preamble, "I want you to tell me a few things, please. You'll excuse me if my questions seem rather pointed, also, if they seem to be queries already answered. Did you kill Mr. Appleby?"

"Yes," said Maida, speaking wearily, as if tired of making the assertion.

"You know no one believes that statement?"

"I can't help that, Mr. Stone," she said, with a listless manner.

"That is, no one but one person—your father. He believes it."

"Father!" exclaimed the girl in evident amazement.

"Yes; he believes you for the best of all possible reasons: He saw you shoot."

"What, Mr. Stone? My father! Saw me shoot Mr. Appleby!"

"Yes; he says so. That is net strange, when, as you say, you fired the pistol from where you stood in the bay window, and Mr. Wheeler stood by or near the victim."

"But—I don't understand. You say, father says he saw me?"

"Yes, he told me that."

Maida was silent, but she was evidently thinking deeply and rapidly.

"This is a trap of some sort, Mr. Stone," she said at last. "My father didn't see me shoot—he couldn't have seen me, and consequently he couldn't say he did! He wouldn't lie about it!"

"But he said, at one time, that he did the shooting himself. Was not that an untruth?"

"Of a quite different sort. He said that in a justifiable effort to save me. But this other matter—for him to say he saw me shoot—when he didn't—he couldn't—"

"Why couldn't he, Miss Wheeler? Why was it so impossible for your father to see you commit that crime, when he was right there?"

"Because—because—oh, Mr. Stone, I don't know what to say! I feel sure I mustn't say anything, or I shall regret it."

"Would you like your father to come here and tell us about it?"

"No;—or, yes. Oh, I don't know. Jeffrey, help me!"

Allen had sat silently brooding all through this conversation. He had not looked at Maida, keeping his gaze turned out of the window. He was sorely hurt at her attitude in the Keefe matter; he was puzzled at her speech regarding her father; and he was utterly uncertain as to his own duty or privilege in the whole affair. But at her appeal, he turned joyfully toward her.

"Oh, Maida," he cried, "let me help you. Do get your father here, now, and settle this question. Then, we'll see what next."

"Call him, then," said Maida, but she turned very white, and paid no further attention to Allen. She was still lost in thought, when her father arrived and joined the group.

"You said, Mr. Wheeler," Stone began at once, "that you saw your daughter fire the shot that killed Mr. Appleby?"

"I did say that," Daniel Wheeler replied, "because it is true. And because I am convinced that the truth will help us all better than any further endeavor to prove a falsehood. I did see you, Maida darling, and I tried very hard to take the blame myself. But it has been proved to me by Mr. Stone that my pretence is useless, and so I've concluded that the fact must come out, in hope of a better result than from concealment. Do not fear, my darling, no harm shall come to you."

"And you said you did it, father, and mother said she did it."

"Yes, of course, I told your mother the truth, and we plotted—yes, plotted for each of us to confess to the deed, in a wild hope of somehow saving our little girl"

"And you saw me shoot, father?"

"Why, yes, dear—that is, I heard the shot, and looked up to see you standing there with consternation and guilt on your dear face. Your arm had then dropped to your side, but your whole attitude was unmistakable. I couldn't shut my eyes to the evident fact that there was no one else who could have done the deed."

"There must have been, father—for—I didn't do it."

"I knew you didn't! Oh, Maida!" With a bound Allen was at her side and his arm went round her. But she moved away from him, and went on talking—still in a strained, unnatural voice, but steadily and straightforwardly.

"No; I didn't shoot Mr. Appleby. I've been saying so, to shield my father. I thought he did it."

"Maida! Is it possible?" and Daniel Wheeler looked perplexed. "But, oh, I'm so glad to hear your statement."

"But who did do it, then?" Miss Lane asked, bluntly.

"Who cares, so long as it wasn't any of the Wheelers!" exclaimed Jeffrey Allen, unable to contain his gladness. "Oh, Maida—"

But again she waved him away from her.

"I don't understand, Mr. Stone," she began; "I don't know where these disclosures will lead. I hope, not back to my mother—"

"No, Maida," said her father, "there's no fear of that."

Reassured, Maida went on. "Perhaps I can't be believed now, after my previous insistence on my guilt, but God knows it is the truth; I am utterly innocent of the crime."

"I believe it," said Fleming Stone. "There was little evidence against you, except your own confession. Now you've retracted that it only remains for me to find the real criminal."

"Can you," cried Fibsy excitedly, "can you, F. Stone?"

"Don't you know which way to look, Terence?"

"I do—and I don't—" the boy murmured; "oh, lordy! I do—and—I don't!"

"But there's another matter to be agreed upon," said Maida, who had not at all regained her normal poise or appearance. Her face was white and her eyes blurred with tears. But she persisted in speech.

"I want it understood that I am engaged to marry Mr. Keefe," she said, not looking at Jeffrey at all. "I announce my engagement, and I desire him to be looked upon and considered as my future husband."

"Maida!" came simultaneously from the lips of her father and Allen.

"Yes, that is positive and irrevocable. I have my own reasons for this, and one of them is "—she paused—" one very important one is, that Mr. Keefe knows who shot Mr. Appleby, and can produce the criminal and guarantee his confession to the deed."

"Wow!" Fibsy remarked, explosively, and Fleming Stone stared at the girl.

"He used this as an argument to persuade you to marry him, Miss Wheeler?"

"I don't put it that way, Mr. Stone, but I have Mr. Keefe's assurance that he will do as I told you, and also that he will arrange to have a full and free pardon granted to my father for the old sentence he is still suffering under."

"Well, Maida, I don't wonder you consented," said Miss Lane, her round eyes wide with surprise. "And I suppose he's going to renounce all claim to this estate?"

"Yes," said Maida, calmly.

"Anything else?" said Allen, unable to keep an ironic note out of his voice.

"Yes," put in Fibsy, "he's going to be governor of Massachusetts."

"Oh, my heavens and earth!" gasped Genevieve, "what rubbish!"

"Rubbish, nothing!" Fibsy defended his statement. "You know he's after it."

"I felt sure he would, when Sam Appleby gave up the running—but—I didn't know he had taken any public steps."

"Never mind what Mr. Keefe is going to do, or not going to do," said Maida, in a tone of finality, "I expect to marry him—and soon."

"Well," said Stone, in a business-like way, "I think our next one to confer with must be Mr. Keefe."

CHAPTER 18: A FINAL CONFESSION

Inquiry for Keefe brought the information that he had gone to a nearby town, but would be back at dinner-time.

Mr. Appleby was also expected to arrive for dinner, coming from home in his motor car.

But in the late afternoon a severe storm set in. The wind rose rapidly and gained great velocity while the rain fell steadily and hard. Curtis Keefe arrived, very wet indeed, though he had protecting clothing. But a telephone message from Sam Appleby said that he was obliged to give up all idea of reaching Sycamore Ridge that night. He had stopped at a roadhouse, and owing to the gale he dared not venture forth again until the storm was over. He would therefore not arrive until next day.

"Lucky we got his word," said Mr. Wheeler. "This storm will soon put many telephone wires out of commission."

When Keefe came down at the dinner hour, he found Maida alone in the living-room, evidently awaiting him.

"My darling!" he exclaimed, going quickly to her side, "my own little girl! Are you here to greet me?"

"Yes," she said, and suffered rather than welcomed his caressing hand on her shoulder. "Curtis, I told them you would tell them who killed Mr. Appleby."

"So I will, dearest, after dinner. Let's not have unpleasant subjects discussed at table. I've been to Rushfield and I've found out all the particulars that I hadn't already learned, and—I've got actual proofs! Now, who's a cleverer detective than the professionals?"

"Then that's all right. Now, are you sure you can also get father freed?"

"I hope to, dear. That's all I can say at present. Do you take me for a magician? I assure you I'm only an ordinary citizen. But I—"

"But you promised—"

"Yes, my little love, I did, and I well know that you promised because I did! Well, I fancy I shall keep every promise I made you, but not every one as promptly as this exposure of the criminal."

"But you'll surely fix it so father can go into Massachusetts—can go to Boston?"

"Well, rather! I expect—though you mustn't say anything about it—but I've an idea that you may yet be a governor's wife! And it wouldn't do then to have your father barred from the state!"

Maida sighed. The hopes Keefe held out were the realization of her dearest wishes—but, oh, the price she must pay! Yet she was strong-willed. She determined to give no thought whatever to Jeffrey, for if she did she knew her purpose would falter. Nor did she even allow herself the doubtful privilege of feeling sorry for him. Well she knew that that way madness lay. And, thought the poor child, sad and broken-hearted though Jeff may be, his sadness and heartbreak are no worse than mine. Not so bad, for I have to take the initiative! I have to take the brunt of the whole situation.

The others assembled, and at dinner no word was said of the tragedy. Save for Maida and Jeffrey Allen, the party was almost a merry one.

Daniel Wheeler and his wife were so relieved at the disclosure of Maida's innocence that they felt they didn't care much what happened next. Fibsy flirted openly with Genevieve and Fleming Stone himself was quietly entertaining.

Later in the evening they gathered in the den and Keefe revealed his discoveries.

"I felt all along," he said, "that there was—there must have been a man on the south veranda who did the shooting. Didn't you think that, Mr. Stone?"

"I did at times," Stone replied, truthfully. "I confess, though my opinion changed once or twice."

"And at the present moment?" insisted Keefe.

"At the present moment, Mr. Keefe, your attitude tells me that you expect to prove that there was such a factor in the case, so I would be foolish indeed to say I doubted it. But, to speak definitely—yes, I do think there was a man there, and he was the murderer. He shot through the window, past Miss Wheeler, and most naturally, her father thought she fired the shot herself. You see, it came from exactly her direction."

"Yes; "agreed Keefe, "and moreover, you remember, Rachel saw the man on the veranda—and the cook also saw him—"

"Yes—the cook saw him!" Fibsy put in, and though the words were innocent enough, his tone indicated a hidden meaning.

But beyond a careless glance, Keefe didn't notice the interruption and went on, earnestly:

"Now, the man the servants saw was the murderer. And I have traced him, found him, and secured his signed confession."

With unconcealed pride in his achievement, Keefe took a folded paper from his pocket and handed it to Daniel Wheeler.

"Why the written confession? Where is the man?" asked Stone, his dark eyes alight with interest.

"Gee!" muttered Fibsy, under his breath, "going some!"

Genevieve Lane stared, round-eyed and excited, while Allen and the Wheelers breathlessly awaited developments.

"John Mills!" exclaimed Mr. Wheeler, looking at the paper. "Oh, the faithful old man! Listen, Stone, this is a signed confession of a man on his death-bed—"

"No longer that," said Keefe, solemnly, "he died this afternoon."

"And signed this just before he died?"

"Yes, Mr. Wheeler. In the hospital. The witnesses, as you see, are the nurses there."

The paper merely stated that the undersigned was the slayer of Samuel Appleby. That the deed was committed in order to free Daniel Wheeler from wicked and unjust molestation and tyranny. The signature, though faintly scrawled, was perfectly legible and duly witnessed.

"He was an old servant of mine," Wheeler said, thoughtfully, "and very devoted to us all. He always resented Appleby's attitude toward me—for Mills was my butler when the trouble occurred, and knew all about it. He has been an invalid for a year, but has been very ill only recently."

"Since the shooting, in fact," said Keefe, significantly.

"It must have been a hard task for one so weak," Wheeler said, "but the old fellow was a true friend to me all his life. Tell us more of the circumstances, Mr. Keefe."

"I did it all by thinking," said Keefe, his manner not at all superior, nor did he look toward Fleming Stone, who was listening attentively. "I felt sure there was some man from outside. And I thought first of some enemy of Mr. Appleby's. But later, I thought it might have been some enemy of Mr. Wheeler's and the shot was possibly meant for him."

Wheeler nodded at this. "I thought that, too," he observed.

"Well, then later, I began to think maybe it was some friend—not an enemy. A friend, of course, of Mr. Wheeler's. On this principle I searched for a suspect. I inquired among the servants, being careful to arouse no suspicion of my real intent. At last, I found this old Mills had always been devoted to the whole family here. More than devoted, indeed. He revered Mr. Wheeler and he fairly worshipped the ladies. He has been ill a long time of a slow and incurable malady, and quite lately was taken to the hospital. When I reached him I saw the poor chap had but a very short time to live."

"And you suspected him of crime with no more evidence than that?" Fleming Stone asked.

"I daresay it was a sort of intuition, Mr. Stone," Keefe returned, smiling a little at the detective. "Oh, I don't wonder you feel rather miffed to have your thunder stolen by a mere business man—and I fear it's unprofessional for me to put the thing through without consulting you, but I felt the case required careful handling—somewhat psychological handling, indeed—"

"Very much so," Stone nodded.

"And so," Keefe was a little disconcerted by the detective's demeanor, but others set it down to a very natural chagrin on Stone's part.

Fibsy sat back in his chair, his bright eyes narrowed to mere slits and darting from the face of Keefe to that of Stone continually.

"And so," Keefe went on, "I inquired from the servants and also, cautiously from the members of the family, and I learned that this Mills was of a fiery, even revengeful, nature—"

"He was," Mr. Wheeler nodded, emphatically.

"Yes, sir. And I found out from Rachel that—"

"Rachel!" Fibsy fairly shot out the word, but a look from Stone made him say no more.

"Yes, Rachel, the maid," went on Keefe, "and I found that the man she saw on the veranda was of the same general size and appearance as Mills. Well, I somehow felt that it was Mills—and so I went to see him."

"At the hospital?" asked Wheeler.

"Yes; some days ago. He was then very weak, and the nurses didn't want me to arouse him to any excitement. But I knew it was my duty—"

"Of course," put in Stone, and Keefe gave him a patronizing look.

"So, against the wishes of the nurses and doctors, I had an interview alone with Mills, and I found he was the criminal."

"He confessed?" asked Stone.

"Yes; and though he refused to sign a written confession, he agreed he would confess in the presence of Mr. Wheeler and Mr. Stone. But—that was only this morning—and the doctor assured me the man couldn't live the day out. So I persuaded the dying man to sign this confession, which I drew up and read to him in the presence of the nurses. He signed—they witnessed—and there it is."

With evident modesty, Keefe pointed to the paper still in Wheeler's hands, and said no more.

For a moment nobody spoke. The storm was at its height. The wind whistled and roared, the rain fell noisily, and the elements seemed to be doing their very worst.

Genevieve shuddered—she always was sensitive to weather conditions, and that wind was enough to disturb even equable nerves.

"And this same Mills was the phantom bugler?" asked Stone.

"Yes—he told me so," returned Keefe. "He knew about the legend, you see, and he thought he'd work on the superstition of the family to divert attention from himself."

Genevieve gasped, but quickly suppressed all show of agitation.

Fibsy whistled—just a few notes of the bugle call that the "phantom "had played.

At the sound Keefe turned quickly, a strange look on his face, and the Wheelers, too, looked startled at the familiar strain.

"Be quiet, Terence," Stone said, rather severely, and the boy subsided.

"Now, Mr. Keefe," Fleming Stone said, "you must not think—as I fear you do—that I grudge admiration for your success, or appreciation of your cleverness. I do not. I tell you, very sincerely, that what you have accomplished is as fine a piece of work as I have ever run across in my whole career as detective. Your intuition was remarkable and your following it up a masterpiece! By the way, I suppose that it was Mills, then, who started the fire in the garage?"

"Yes, it was," said Keefe. "You see, he is a clever genius, in a sly way. He reasoned that if a fire occurred, everybody would run to it except Mr. Wheeler, who cannot go over the line. He hoped that, therefore, Mr. Appleby would not go either—for Mr. Appleby suffered from flatfoot—at any rate, he took a chance that the fire would give him opportunity to shoot unnoticed. Which it did."

"It certainly did. Now, Mr. Keefe, did he tell you how he set that fire?"

"No, he did not," was the short reply. "Moreover, Mr. Stone, I resent your mode of questioning. I'm not on the witness stand. I've solved a mystery that baffled you, and though I understand your embarrassment at the situation, yet it does not give you free rein to make what seem to me like endeavors to trip me up!"

"Trip you up!" Stone lifted his eyebrows. "What a strange expression to use. As if I suspected you of faking his tale."

"It speaks for itself," and Keefe glanced nonchalantly at the paper he had brought. "There's the signed confession—if you can prove that signature a fake—go ahead."

"No," said Daniel Wheeler, decidedly; "that's John Mills' autograph. I know it perfectly. He wrote that himself. And a dying man is not going to sign a lie. There's no loophole of doubt, Mr. Stone. I think you must admit Mr. Keefe's entire success."

"I do admit Mr. Keefe's entire success," Stone's dark eyes flashed, "up to this point. From here on, I shall undertake to prove my own entire success, since that is the phrase we are using. Mr. Wheeler, your present cook was here when John Mills worked for you?"

"She was, Mr. Stone, but you don't need her corroboration of this signature. I tell you I know it to be Mills'."

"Will you send for the cook, please?"

Half unwillingly, Wheeler agreed, and Maida stepped out of the room and summoned the cook.

The woman came in, and Stone spoke to her at once.

"Is that John Mills' signature?" he asked, showing her the paper.

"It is, sir," she replied, looking at him in wonder.

A satisfied smile played on Keefe's face, only to be effaced at Stone's next question.

"And was John Mills the person you saw—vaguely—on the south veranda that night of Mr. Appleby's murder?"

"That he was not!" she cried, emphatically. "It was a man not a bit like Mills, and be the same token, John Mills was in his bed enable to walk at all, at all."

"That will do, Mr. Wheeler," and Stone dismissed the cook with a glance. "Now, Mr. Keefe?"

"As if that woman's story mattered," Keefe sneered, contemptuously, "she is merely mistaken, that's all. The word of the maid, Rachel, is as good as that of the cook—"

"Oh, no, it isn't!" Stone interrupted, but, paying no heed to him, Keefe went on; "and you can scarcely doubt the signature after Mr. Wheeler and your friend the cook have both verified it."

Though his demeanor was quiet, Keefe's face wore a defiant expression and his voice was a trifle blustering.

"I do not doubt the signature," Stone declared, "nor do I doubt that you obtained it at the hospital exactly as you have described that incident."

Keefe's face relaxed at that, and he recovered his jaunty manner, as he said: "Then you admit I have beaten you at your own game, Mr. Stone?"

"No, Mr. Keefe, but I have beaten you at yours."

A silence fell for a moment. There was something about Stone's manner of speaking that made for conviction in the minds of his hearers that he said truth.

"Wait a minute! Oh, wait a minute!" It was Genevieve Lane who cried out the words, and then she sprang from her chair and ran to Keefe's side.

Flinging her arms about him, she whispered close to his ear.

He listened, and then, with a scornful gesture he flung her off.

"No!" he said to her; "no! a thousand times, no! Do your worst."

"I shall!" replied Genevieve, and without another word she resumed her seat.

"Yes," went on Stone, this interruption being over, "your ingenious 'success' in the way of detecting is doomed to an ignominious end. You see, sir," he turned to Daniel Wheeler, "the clever ruse Mr. Keefe has worked, is but a ruse—a stratagem, to deceive us, all and to turn the just suspicion of the criminal in an unjust direction."

"Explain, Mr. Stone," said Wheeler, apparently not much impressed with what he deemed a last attempt on the part of the detective to redeem his reputation.

"Yes, Mr. Stone," said Keefe, "if my solution of this mystery is a ruse—a stratagem—what have you to offer in its place? You admit the signed confession?"

"I admit the signature, but not the confession. John Mills signed that paper, Mr. Keefe, but he is not the murderer."

"Who is, then?"

"You are!"

Keefe laughed and shrugged his shoulders, but at that moment there was such a blast of wind and storm, accompanied by a fearful crash, that what he said could not be heard.

"Explain, please, Mr. Stone," Wheeler said again, after a pause, but his voice now showed more interest.

"I will. The time has come for it. Mr. Wheeler, do you and Mr. Allen see to it, that Mr. Keefe does not leave the room. Terence—keep your eyes open."

Keefe still smiled, but his smile was a frozen one. His eyes began to widen and his hands clenched themselves upon his knees.

"Curtis Keefe killed Samuel Appleby," Stone went on, speaking clearly but rapidly. "His motive was an ambition to be governor of Massachusetts. He thought that with the elder Appleby out of the way, his son would have neither power nor inclination to make a campaign. There were other, minor motives, but that was his primary one. That, and the fact that the elder Appleby had a hold on Mr. Keefe, and of late had pressed it home uncomfortably hard. The murder was long premeditated. The trip here brought it about, because it offered a chance where others might reasonably be suspected. Keefe was the man on the veranda, whom the cook saw—but not clearly enough to distinguish his identity. Though she did know it was not John Mills."

"But—Mr. Stone "interrupted Wheeler, greatly perturbed, "think what you're saying! Have you evidence to prove your statements?"

"I have, Mr. Wheeler, as you shall see. Let me tell my story and judge me then. A first proof is—Terence, you may tell of the bugle."

"I went, at Mr. Stone's orders," the boy stated, pimply, "to all the shops or little stores in this vicinity where a bugle might have been bought; I found one was bought in a very small shop in Rushfield and bought by a man who corresponded to Mr. Keefe's description, and who, when he stopped at the shop, was in a motor car whose description and occupants were the Appleby bunch. Well, anyway—Miss Lane here knows that Mr. Keefe bought that bugle—don't you?" He turned to Genevieve, who, after a glance at Keefe, nodded affirmation.

"And so," Stone went on, "Mr. Keefe used that bugle—"

"How did he get opportunity?" asked Wheeler.

"I'll tell you," offered Genevieve. "We all staid over night in Rushfield, and I heard Mr. Keefe go out of doors in the night. I watched him from my window. He returned about three hours later."

It was clear to all listening, that when Genevieve had whispered to Keefe and he had told her to do her worst, they were now hearing the "worst."

"So," Stone narrated, "Mr. Keefe came over here and did the bugling as a preliminary to his further schemes. You admit that, Mr. Keefe?"

"I admit nothing. Tell your silly story as you please."

"I will. Then, the day of the murder, Mr. Keefe arranged for the fire in the garage. He used the acids as the man Fulton described, and as Keefe's own coat was burned and his employer's car he felt sure suspicion would not turn toward him. When the fire broke out—which as it depended on the action of those acids, he was waiting for, Keefe ran with Mr. Allen to the garage. But—and this I have verified from Mr. Allen, Keefe disappeared for a moment, and, later was again at Allen's side. In that moment—Mr. Wheeler, that psychological moment, Curtis Keefe shot and killed Samuel Appleby."

"And Mills?"

"Is part of the diabolically clever scheme. Mills was dying; he was leaving a large family without means of support. He depended, and with reason, on hope of your generosity, Mr. Wheeler, to his wife and children. But Curtis Keefe went to him and told him that you were about to be dispossessed of your home and fortune, and that if he would sign the confession—knowing what it was—that he, Keefe, would settle a large sum of money on Mrs. Mills and the children at once. And he did."

"You fiend! You devil incarnate!" cried Keefe, losing all control. "How do you know that?"

"I found it all out from Mrs. Mills," Stone replied; "your accomplices all betrayed you, Mr. Keefe. A criminal should beware of accomplices. Rachel turned state's evidence and told how you bribed her to make up that story of the bugler—or rather, to relate parrot-like—the story you taught to her."

"It's all up," said Keefe, flinging out his hands in despair. "You've outwitted me at every point, Mr. Stone. I confess myself vanquished—"

"And you confess yourself the murderer?" said Stone, quickly.

"I do, but I ask one favor. May I take that paper a moment?"

"Certainly," said Stone, glancing at the worthless confession.

Keefe stepped to the table desk, where the paper lay, but as he laid his left hand upon it, with his right he quickly pulled open a drawer, grasped the pistol that was in it, and saying, with a slight smile: "A life for a life!" drew the trigger and fell to the floor.

From the gruesome situation, its silence made worse by the noise of the storm outside, Daniel Wheeler led his wife and daughter. Jeffrey Allen followed quickly and sought his loved Maida.

Reaction from the strain made her break down, and sobbing in his arms she asked and received full forgiveness for her enforced desertion of him.

"I couldn't do anything else, Jeff," she sobbed. "I had to say yes to him for dad's sake—and mother's."

"Of course you did, darling; don't think about it. Oh, Maida, look! The wind has torn up the sycamore! Unrooted it, and it has fallen over—"

"Over into Massachusetts!" Maida cried; "Jeffrey, think what that means!"

"Why—why!" Allen was speechless.

"Yes; the sycamore has gone into Massachusetts—and father can go!"

"Is that real, Maida—is it truly a permission?"

"Of course it is! We've got Governor Appleby's letter, saying so—written when he was governor, you know! Jeffrey—I'm so happy! It makes me forget that awful—"

"Do forget it all you can, dearest," and beneath her lover's caresses, Maida did forget, for the moment at least.

"It's the only inexplicable thing about it all, Fibs," Fleming Stone observed, after the case was among the annals of the past, "that the old sycamore fell over and fell the right way."

"Mighty curious, F. Stone," rejoined the boy, with an expressionless face.

"You didn't help it along, did you? You know the injunction was, 'without intervention of human hands'—"

"I didn't intervent my hands, Mr. Stone," said the boy, earnestly, "honest I didn't. But—it wasn't nominated in the bond that I shouldn't kick around those old decaying roots with my foot—just so's if it should take a notion to fall it would fall heading north!"

THE END

RESURRECTED PRESS CLASSIC MYSTERY CATALOGUE

E. C. Bentley
Trent's Last Case: The Woman in Black

Ernest Bramah
Max Carrados Resurrected:
The Detective Stories of Max Carrados

Agatha Christie
The Secret Adversary
The Mysterious Affair at Styles

Octavus Roy Cohen
Midnight

Freeman Wills Croft
The Ponson Case
The Pit Prop Syndicate

J. S. Fletcher
The Herapath Property
The Rayner-Slade Amalgamation
The Chestermarke Instinct
The Paradise Mystery
Dead Men's Money
The Middle of Things
Ravensdene Court
Scarhaven Keep
The Orange-Yellow Diamond
The Middle Temple Murder
The Tallyrand Maxim
The Borough Treasurer
In the Mayor's Parlour
The Safety Pin
R. Austin Freeman

The Mystery of 31 New Inn from the Dr. Thorndyke Series
John Thorndyke's Cases from the Dr. Thorndyke Series
The Red Thumb Mark from The Dr. Thorndyke Series
The Eye of Osiris from The Dr. Thorndyke Series
A Silent Witness from the Dr. John Thorndyke Series
The Cat's Eye from the Dr. John Thorndyke Series
Helen Vardon's Confession: A Dr. John Thorndyke Story
As a Thief in the Night: A Dr. John Thorndyke Story
Mr. Pottermack's Oversight: A Dr. John Thorndyke Story
Dr. Thorndyke Intervenes: A Dr. John Thorndyke Story
The Singing Bone: The Adventures of Dr. Thorndyke
The Stoneware Monkey: A Dr. John Thorndyke Story
The Great Portrait Mystery, and Other Stories: A Collection of Dr. John Thorndyke and Other Stories
The Penrose Mystery: A Dr. John Thorndyke Story
The Uttermost Farthing: A Savant's Vendetta

Arthur Griffiths
The Passenger From Calais
The Rome Express

Fergus Hume
The Mystery of a Hansom Cab
The Green Mummy
The Silent House
The Secret Passage

Edgar Jepson
The Loudwater Mystery

A. E. W. Mason
At the Villa Rose

A. A. Milne
The Red House Mystery

Baroness Emma Orczy
The Old Man in the Corner

Edgar Allan Poe
The Detective Stories of Edgar Allan Poe

Arthur J. Rees
The Hampstead Mystery
The Shrieking Pit
The Hand In The Dark
The Moon Rock
The Mystery of the Downs

Mary Roberts Rinehart
Sight Unseen and The Confession

Dorothy L. Sayers
Whose Body?

Sir William Magnay
The Hunt Ball Mystery

Mabel and Paul Thorne
The Sheridan Road Mystery

Louis Tracy
The Strange Case of Mortimer Fenley
The Albert Gate Mystery
The Bartlett Mystery
The Postmaster's Daughter
The House of Peril
The Sandling Case: What Would You Have Done?
Charles Edmonds Walk
The Paternoster Ruby

Mildred A. Wirt
The Clock Strikes Thirteen
Clue of the Silken Ladder
The Cry at Midnight
Ghost Beyond the Gate
Guilt of the Brass Thieves
Hoofbeats on the Turnpike
The Secret Pact
Saboteurs on the River
Signal in the Dark
Voice from the Cave
Whispering Walls
The Wishing Well

And much more!
Visit ResurrectedPress.com for our complete catalogue

About Resurrected Press

A division of Intrepid Ink, LLC, Resurrected Press is dedicated to bringing high quality, vintage books back into publication. See our entire catalogue and find out more at www.ResurrectedPress.com.

About Intrepid Ink, LLC

Intrepid Ink, LLC provides full publishing services to authors of fiction and non-fiction books, eBooks and websites. From editing to formatting, from publishing to marketing, Intrepid Ink gets your creative works into the hands of the people who want to read them. Find out more at www.IntrepidInk.com.